KAPS

BOOK FIVE OF THE ANGELBOUND OFFSPRING SERIES

CHRISTINA BAUER

COPYRIGHT

Monster House Books
Brighton, MA 02135
ISBN 9781945723568
First Edition

DEDICATION

For All Those Who Kick Ass, Take Names
And Read Books

PREFACE

KAPS begins with an expanded version of the epilogue club scene from the previous novel, RHODES.

KAPS

KAPS

Sometimes, you simply must punch a shape-shifting vampire Nazi.

Like tonight, for instance.

I stroll through New York's Central Park. Ahead of me, there strides a guy in a chicken costume. I'm talking yellow feathers, plumed tail, the whole smash. A sash extends from his shoulder to his hip that reads *Eat At Cluck Town*. This fellow is anything but normal, and not for the obvious wardrobe reasons.

He's actually a vampire.

Even worse, he's an audax, which is a shape-shifting vampire Nazi. All audax started off as German soldiers in World War II. During a raid, they entered the magical city of El Dorado, got changed into vampires, and have been causing trouble ever since.

All of which is why I can't wait to punch this particular blood sucker.

With a stake.

Right through his heart.

Because I'm more than just a teenager who's dressed up for a night of dancing. I'm a dragon-shifter princess with a secret obsession.

Slaying audax.

I know. My life is strange. It runs in the family.

Squinting, I focus on the guy's birdy outfit. Dragon shifters like me are immune to supernatural glamours, so I can easily detect the decaying body that's magically hidden under all those feathers.

Hello, vampire.

The real costume-wearing human got attacked by an audax. After drinking the victim's blood, this particular vampire magically took on the man's appearance, bird outfit and all.

And the *original* chicken guy? Way dead.

Cold sorrow moves through me. Most likely, I'm the first to know about this lost life. I'm certainly the only one around here who detects the audax.

Ah, to be a clueless human. They've no idea how many evils surround them.

For his part, Vampire Chicken Guy (VCG for short) keeps sauntering along the stone path, his plumed tail bobbing with each step. He pulls off his fake chicken head to reveal someone my age—that would be seventeen—with round cheeks, short red hair and tons of freckles. *A stolen face.*

My grief melts into lava-hot rage. *How dare this audax kill a human?* I twist the clunky golden bracelet around my right wrist. If I take this off and flip the segments about, it transforms into a small spike. That's the only way to fully kill an audax…

A golden stake through the heart.

Meanwhile VCG smiles innocently at passersby. New Yorkers actually grin and wave in return, which is rare. *Must be a chicken thing.* I hoist up my bandeau top and keep following. The dance club can wait.

VCG is going down.

My prey slips off into a cluster of trees. Adrenaline courses through my bloodstream. Whipping off my bracelet, I convert the jewelry into a mini-stake. This size isn't as powerful as my regular weapon, but it'll get the job done. With every step, my tail sways behind me in a predatory rhythm. It's invisible to humans while being covered in dragon scales. *Super useful in a fight.*

I step into a small clearing—the same secluded nook that VCG just entered—and carefully scan my new surroundings.

There are trees.

Greenery.

And a random tortoise.

My heart sinks. No VCG.

Ring, ring...

I pull out my cell phone and see the familiar image of my sister, Huntress, on the screen. As always, Huntress carries an aristocratic air that says, *you shall follow me NOW.* It's her mix of fine features, violet eyes and oodles of confidence. By contrast, I have brown hair and eyes, as well as a vibe that screams, *I'm uncomfortable in my own skin.* Which is true.

Before answering, I take a moment to change character. Just now, I was playing the Lone Vigilante, a version of myself that fights vampires solo. When chatting with my sister, I must toss my Lone Vigilante self aside and become a new character, the Family Fuck Up. Because if folks knew about my Lone Vigilante antics, then I'd be locked up in a tower forever. No joke. My family's nutso when it comes to safety.

I pop in my earpiece. "Hey, Huntress."

"Ready for tonight's mission?"

A nearby shrub catches my attention. My Lone Vigilante instantly rises to the surface. *Maybe that shrub holds a clue about where VCG slunk off to.*

"Did you hear me?" asks Huntress.

"Uh, what was that again?" To play the Family Fuck

Up, it's always important to stammer while asking dumbass questions.

"I was talking about tonight's mission," repeats Huntress. "Are you ready?"

A spot of yellow catches my eye. *Ah-HA!* That might be a feather. I step closer and indeed, I discover something colorful.

A Butterfinger wrapper. *Bummer.*

"Mission for what?" This time, I take care to imagine my head as full of cotton candy.

I can almost hear Huntress roll her eyes. "The Wurtzite dagger."

"Oh yeah. *That* mission."

Huntress clears her throat. "Here's the rundown for tonight, in case you forgot."

In other words, Huntress totally thinks I forgot.

In truth, I can recite every detail for tonight from memory. The Lone Vigilante forgets nothing.

"I'll start with the target," continues Huntress. "It's a human male named Mack. Over six feet tall. Strong build. Blue eyes. Nineteen years old. Tonight he'll be carrying a Wurtzite dagger, which is a magical blade that can cut through anything."

Originally, Huntress and I needed the Wurtzite dagger to protect my twin, Zinnia. But Zin is totally safe these days. Now the Lone Vigilante wants the weapon because MAGICAL DAGGER.

Huntress keeps going. "According to my intel, Mack is due at La Vida tonight. Do you know the place?"

"Yup. I've hit that club before. Good dance spot."

"Oh, this is interesting," adds Huntress. "It says here, Mack is also part of the zoetic, a group of humans who fight something called the audax."

Now I could volunteer a ton of audax info at this point, but I won't. As far as my family is concerned, I'm a crackpot who loves touring Earth with my (arguably awful) rock band.

Yes, I'm living a lie. The rock band is just a cover. I only book gigs where there are vampires to kill or magical relics to uncover. And sure, it's kind of lonely. I juggle so many masks, I don't know which one is really me, if any.

At least I don't cry myself to sleep. I'm more of a *whimper and eat popcorn before bedtime* kind of girl.

A rustle sounds in the nearby trees. *Can that be VCG?* I pause.

Static crackles over my earpiece. "Do you know anything about the zoetic?" asks Huntress.

I step closer to the noisy tree. "One sec," I whisper.

"Hey," snaps Huntress. "Are you stalking someone?"

Wow. Leave it to Huntress to detect stalking behavior

over the phone. She's well named, by the way. This girl can track anyone, anywhere.

"No, I'm just testing out this new..." I search for something that a fellow dragon shifter would believe. "Human exercise craze. You have to whisper while, uh, jogging."

Not my best lie.

"Exercise?" Huntress' voice takes on a decidedly skeptical note. "But you don't work out. Dragon shifters are naturally strong."

"Eh, you know me. Always trying crazy human stuff just for the fun of it."

"Oh." *And that's all Huntress needs to say.* My reputation as a nut job does the rest.

In the background, a palace servant asks something about a busted pipe. "Let me check," Huntress says to the servant. To me she asks: "Can you wait a sec?"

"No problem."

I tiptoe even closer to the tree. There's not much to see, unless you count bark and a few crawly things. By comparison, the Butterfinger wrapper seems like a great find. As a matter of fact, I'm about to give up the search when it happens.

VCG falls from the branches above.

And lands right on my head.

I get knocked to my stomach with a vampire chicken

crouching on my back. Since his headgear is still off, the vamp leans in and licks my ear.

Eew.

"How fortunate that I shall kill you now," snarls the vampire. "If you sought out the Halcyon coven, then you'd die in a far more painful way."

Huh. In truth, I have zero plans to seek out the Halcyon witches. That said, I've always been interested in the Halcyons—mostly because they're somewhat related to the audax. And the fact that I'm being warned away from them?

Death be damned. Now I'm totally hunting the Halycons down.

After I kick this vampire's ass, obviously.

2

MACK

I stand in a long stone room filled with cots. *The Zoetic Healing Chamber.* Small square windows line the walls, casting pale columns of light onto the floor. Three-hundred and four zoetic operatives lie here in neat rows. Every last one of them is unconscious.

None are healing.

We zoetic slay shape-shifting vampires. In our line of work, magical illnesses are a common risk. In the past, we've always healed from supernatural sickness.

Until a year ago. That's when the first zoetic fell into an enchanted sleep. And this isn't a magical snooze of the Snow White variety. Those who are struck down face a slow and painful death. All we can do is reduce their pain.

These days, our numbers are few. Zoetic who haven't fallen ill have run off. Not that I blame them. No one knows why zoetic are getting sick in the first place. Why hang around to be the next victim?

I scan the nearby cots. Familiar faces catch my attention. There's Callista from our League of Bounty Hunters. Patariki the assassin. Mairwen of the Relic Masters. And Ndidi, the finest spy in our Cabal of Ghosts.

He's also my best friend.

I pause beside Ndidi's cot. Crimson mist shifts across his skin, clouding over his wide eyes, dark complexion and defined bone structure. It's this magical haze that keeps my friend asleep while it slowly takes his life.

Memories churn. I picture Ndidi and I training together as kids. Fighting side by side as adults. And always sharing a good laugh at bad jokes. Now I have no way to help him.

Bracing my shoulders, I wait for rage and sorrow to stab through me.

Nothing happens.

In truth, I haven't felt a twinge of feeling in months. Only emptiness. Ndidi warned me about this. He's always concerned for the welfare of others.

Pain is fire, Ndidi said. *If you aren't careful, it can burn out your soul.*

Seems he was right.

Our lead medic, Felix, steps up beside me. He's a stout guy in scrubs with unruly black hair and an easy smile. By contrast, I'm in my standard outfit: jeans and a black T.

"You never miss visiting hours, do you, Mako?" asks Felix.

"Try not to."

Actually, my name is Mack. The Mako nickname started six months ago, right when this hollowness settled into my heart. The fact that Felix calls me Mako —which is a type of shark—is meant as a complement. Other zoetic believe I'm a coldhearted predator who keeps going no matter what.

Felix lifts a small handheld from the pocket of his blue scrubs. "I used the Spyglass of Tierney to check Ndidi last night." He flicks through some screens. "Your friend's bloom levels should be in here somewhere."

The bloom. That's what we call the rose-colored haze that keeps my friend in a magical sleep. It's a nice name for a horrific illness.

Felix is one hundred percent human, so he can't see the layers of crimson magic that move across Ndidi's body.

Yet I can.

There's a dash of demonic DNA in my heritage, so I

detect the supernatural side of things without needing magical relics like the Spyglass of Tierney. Every day, I see stuff like demons, vampires and enchantments. In fact, I can even observe the worry tick that's gnawing on Felix's ear. It's a small demon that feeds off anxiety.

"Where *is* that screen?" Felix pulls on his earlobe, making the demon hop straight over his head, only to land on his other ear.

"You still have that worry demon."

Felix looks up, his eyes wide. "Are you sure?"

"Yeah." I crack my knuckles. "You want it gone? It won't hurt much."

Felix gasps. I shouldn't have said the *hurt much* part.

"No," replies Felix quickly. "I'm starting another herbal cleanse. This one will do the trick."

I shrug. I've already told Felix that you can't expel a worry tick without pain. But the medic has his own ideas.

Felix taps his screen. "Ah, here it is. There's hardly any bloom on Ndidi. Just a few spots here and there."

"Things have changed," I state, my voice low and calm. "The enchantment's all over him now. Ndidi's getting worse."

Felix pales. "And you aren't upset?"

"I am what you see." *Empty.*

Felix stares at me, his mouth hanging open with shock. "You really are a Mako."

He's not wrong. I gesture toward the data pad. "How about updating Ndidi's chart?"

"Sure, sure." Felix quickly types onto his data pad. Taking in a deep breath, the medic forces a smile. I've seen this move before. Felix wants to make some small talk and ease the situation. Not sure that's possible.

"You must be so excited," offers Felix.

"For what?"

"The other paladins."

Paladins like me have mastered all four zoetic orders: the League of Bounty Hunters, Order of Assassins, Relic Masters, and Cabal of Ghosts.

"Not sure what you mean."

"Next week, all the other paladins return from their retreat. Another paladin told me about it. You must be thrilled."

"Ace was the one who told you, right?" He's the only other paladin left. He also happens to be a scheming douchebag.

"Sure, Ace said the retreat was held in Scotland or something."

"Hmm."

Not sure what else to say. Truth is, there are no other

paladins on retreat. It's just me and Ace these days—everyone else on our level is sick or run off.

"The paladins *do* return next week, right?" asks Felix.

The guy looks so hopeful, I can't be the one to burst his bubble. "Sure."

"Great news," says Felix. "See you later."

As Felix steps away, the main door to the healing chamber swings open. My Zoetic Liege, Roman, steps through. He's my height with a sinewy build. As always, Roman wears a white lab coat. He has unkempt gray hair, small round glasses, and a manic look in his silver eyes. Overall, he reminds me of a hyperactive Albert Einstein.

Roman raises his hand in greeting. "Eureka!"

I bow as he approaches. "My Liege."

"No formal nonsense today. I have found the cure for the bloom. Eureka!"

Roman often locks himself in his lab for weeks. By repeatedly saying *eureka*, my Liege means he has a new discovery to share. About half of these ideas are brilliant. The other fifty percent? *Ah, no.*

I fold my arms over my chest. "What is it?"

Roman grins. "We'll get the Essence."

Huh.

"Let me get this straight," I say slowly. "You'll cure the bloom by getting the Essence, which is a magical potion that can heal anything. Plus, the serum can only created by the Halcyon coven, a group of super-powerful witches who probably don't exist."

"Precisely! It's so simple and perfect, I don't know why I didn't see it before!"

That's Roman for you. One time, he wanted all zoetic to drink a potion so we could develop a third eye. Literally.

Roman pulls some crumpled documents from the pocket of his lab coat. "Remember that vial Ace found last month?"

"From the Black Lotus coven. It was all dried out. Maybe a drop of potion left?"

"That's the one." Roman presses the papers into my hands. "It's all in these documents. I reconstituted the liquid. The Black Lotus didn't brew that serum. The magical signature says Halcyon."

I scan the analysis in my hands, which resembles nothing more than a mishmash of letters. But if you read every fifth one, the words become clear. I read them aloud. "Property of the Halcyon coven." I lift my brows. "I'll be damned."

"And look what this potion does." Roman shoves more pages in my direction.

I inspect the new sheets. In these tests, just a fraction

of a droplet eats through almost any pathogen. "Wow. This serum *does* act like the Essence."

"The Halcyons are real. So is the Essence. No one's better at uncovering supernatural artifacts than you, Mack. You'll soon discover a magical relic that leads to both the Halcyons and the Essence. I know it."

"All right, Roman." I set my hand on his shoulder. "I'll try."

With that, I saunter off, cell phone in hand. In cases like this, there's only one group to call.

The dragon shifter mafia.

3

KAPS

*a*fter VCG knocks me to the ground, we wrestle and fight for *who knows how long*. There's a lot of hissing and baring of teeth, that's for sure. As we get into the rhythm of battle, the blur of activity narrows into a series of quick movements. Each one's like turning the page in a book.

VCG pins me.

I flip him.

VCG punches.

I duck.

VCG jams his feathery elbow onto my breast.

Not cool.

So I kick him right in the nuts. Even as a vampire, that's gotta hurt. VCG winces but doesn't topple to the ground.

Mental note: Vampire Chicken Guy has a high tolerance for dick pain.

We're circling each other when Huntress' voice crackles over my earpiece again. "I'm back. What time should we meet up at the club? I'm thinking 1AM."

Damn, I forgot about my call with Huntress.

"Cool," I say quickly.

"You didn't agree," warns Huntress.

Sadly, my sister totally knows my system. Unless I specifically say I'll be somewhere at a certain time, it'll never happen. And even when I do commit, it isn't a lock. What can I say? Audax murder opportunities always seem to come up when I least expect it.

"Gotta go," I add. *Which is true.*

Tapping my earpiece, I end the call while giving VCG a roundhouse kick to the head. It's like punting a concrete pylon. Not much happens.

This audax is pretty strong, which is gross. It means he's chugged a ton of human blood over the years. Very senior vampires get extra magical abilities too. Best to stay alert.

My mind races through options. I could change into my dragon form, but that will flatten this group of trees. Humans are sure to notice the damaged greenery, even if they don't see the bulky creature that caused it in the first place.

And if humans take an interest, they crack out cell phones and authorities. Things get complicated.

All of this boils down to a single fact: I'm not a great warrior. I always skip battle training. And strategy and tactics courses. And fire breathing classes. You get the idea. I have the raw materials to become a fighter, but *meh* in the motivation department.

In moments like this, that seems like a big miss.

Then I recall what I have spent lots of time on: *being a sneaky little bitch.* It goes with playing different characters.

An idea appears. I have a nifty dragonscale tail. Humans can't see it, but it's handy as Hell. Plus, that random tortoise still hangs out nearby. Combine the two and I can slay this vampire.

I scoop up my shelled friend from the ground. Using my tail, I angle open the turtle's beak. Lunging forward, I clamp said beak right onto the VCG's already-sore nut sack. This time, the vampire moans while falling over.

Sneaky little bitch for the win!

Whipping out my handy mini-stake, I punch the audax right through the heart.

Take that, Vampire Chicken Guy.

Golden light encircles VCG. Once again, it's an effect that only supernaturals can detect. The chicken costume fades with a flare of enchanted brightness. When the glow is gone, so is the poultry look.

At this point, I take care to safely remove the tortoise. There are some things even wild animals don't need to see.

Now a man in a Nazi uniform lies on the ground before me. I'm not gonna lie—this part of vampire slaying always gives me the creeps. Audax were created from Nazi soldiers in World War II. And based on the state of this one's outfit, he hasn't washed his uniform since.

Not that it matters. The rest of this Nazi is also a mess. As in, the guy's decaying corpse is missing huge chunks of flesh. Shards of bone poke through the tears in his jacket. One eye dangles from its socket.

The audax clutches at his chest. "The Elector will kill you."

I pinch my fingers and thumb together, miming the motion of someone talking. "Yeah, yeah."

Before audax die, they always *blah-blah-blah* about how their all-powerful leader, the Elector, will destroy me.

Whatever.

This one gets extra chatty. "Now you shall seek out the Halcyon coven."

I purse my lips. *He's back on the Halcyons.* That's a

really good idea, actually. The Halcyons supposedly entered the magical city of El Dorado right around the time as the first audax. While Nazis left the city as vampires, the Halcyons departed as experts in potions.

It could all be a pack of lies, of course. *Or not.* In any case, it's just a matter of uncovering the right magical relics. Then I can suss out the truth, one way or another.

"Appreciate the reminder," I say to the vampire. "Consider the Halcyon coven on my *to do* list."

"Then that quest shall be your destruction!"

The vampire erupts with another blaze of golden fire. Once the flames die down, the audax corpse is nothing but a pile of ash. A breeze sweeps the remnants away.

Killing a vampire? Done.

Finding the mysterious Halcyon coven? Very much on the list.

And getting myself a Wurtzite dagger? That's up next.

4

MACK

ime to chat up the shifter mafia.

I step out of the healing chamber and into a secluded nook. Once I'm sure no one else is around, I press the speed dial code for Gage Beaumont, King of the L'Griffe syndicate. Gage leads the largest dragon shifter mafia on Earth.

"Mack, how good of you to call." Gage has a raspy voice with a French accent. "I was just thinking about you."

"Really?"

"I've already set up a job for you tonight. Word is out. You're going on a bounty hunter mission. Zee payout is quite large." With Gage's accent, words like *the* always sound like *zee*.

That catches my attention. "I'm not interested in cash,

but I might take the gig in return for the right information." *Here's my chance.* "What do you know about the Halcyon coven?"

"Halcyons gained their power from the magical city of El Dorado, same as audax. Rumors are, zee coven lives to this day."

I knew Gage would be the right guy.

"I need to find them. Where's their den?"

"No idea. But they give strong visions to artists."

It's well known that the Halcyons inspired many paintings and songs over the years. "How would that help?"

"Some artists funnel off magic from the supernatural. I've one relic in my collection that I think contains genuine power from the Halcyons. It could lead you to their den. I can provide directions to acquire zee relic, but my bounty hunter mission must completed first. Tonight."

The way the zoetic system works, bounty hunters track down vampires and tag them for death. Then someone from the Order of Assassins does the actual slaying. Seems like Gage wants a particular vampire brought in. That way, the L'Griffe can do the killing themselves. *Simple enough.*

"Which audax is your target?" I ask.

"I'm not after a vampire."

"Then what am I hunting down?"

"I have a bounty out on a non-audax. Deliver them to me and I will give you directions to acquire zee relic."

"I don't go after humans."

"Not a problem. This target's a dragon shifter." There's a certain overly-sweet lilt in the way Gage says the words *not a problem.* He's definitely hiding something.

"And?" I prompt.

"She's—"

"Wait, *she*? I do *not* hunt down girls." Audax are all men, which suits me fine.

"But this princess is a menace. She steals magical relics from us. It must stop."

"Two are things I don't like about this gig. One, you want this done tonight. And two, you just used the word *princess.*"

"Your target is Kappa Psi Phi Sigma, Princess of Furonium. Did I not mention that before?"

"No, you did not."

"Does it bother you?"

"The royalty part doesn't. Neither does the dragon shifter stuff. But the fact that my target is a girl? That's over the line." I rub my neck. "I'll see if Ace can step in tonight."

"Put him on your team if you like. But you know Ace isn't up to this kind of mission."

Which is true. Ace is good for scheming in corners and lying to guys like Felix. Other than that, I haven't seen him do much in terms of actual field work.

"Tonight, zee princess will visit a Manhattan club called La Vida. She thinks you'll arrive with a magical weapon called a Wurtzite dagger. As I told you, she collects supernatural relics. Wurtzite will be your lure." Clicks sound in the background. Gage must be at his computer. "I just sent you encrypted files with all details."

My phone dings as a Gage's message comes in. For a moment, all I can do is stare at the alert. My heart sinks. *Taking the princess to L'Griffe is wrong, pure and simple.*

I open my mouth, ready to say just that. Then I picture Ndidi. No question about it. My friend is succumbing quickly to the *bloom.* For that matter, so is everyone else in the healing chamber.

I must find a cure.

Sometimes, you only get a choice of evils. I'm a paladin because I can make the final call. And in this case? The princess is just one person, while this mission will save hundreds of lives.

"Fine," I announce. "I'll make it happen."

5

KAPS

*T*hump, *thump, thump.*

I wait inside Club Nova. Techno music blares in my ears. Lights flash. Humans dance, oblivious to the demons around them. Some folks have crimson monkey demons hanging off their backs or perched on their shoulders. Others have red vanity bugs all over their faces. These monsters are invisible to humans, but clear enough to me.

With every passing minute, fresh anxiety pulses through my limbs, and it's not from the nearby demons. Questions ricochet through my mind.

Where's this Mack guy?

Why's it taking so long?

Is this even the right club?

A while ago, I got a text from Huntress that

explained how Mack was hitting Club Nova instead of La Vida. But hours have passed since then.

Maybe I should switch to La Vida instead.

Once the idea hits me, I dismiss it. Huntress is never wrong. As a matter of fact, it's annoying how correct she can be.

Speaking of Huntress, my cell buzzes against my hip once more. I don't need to check the device. Without a doubt, my sister is texting me for a firm time to meet.

Not happening.

My sister Zinnia was kidnapped as a kid. Zin's free now, but the aftershocks linger. Long story short, if my family knew I had a vampire slaying obsession, they'd lock me up in the tower and toss the key. It's a nice tower, but still.

Audax need killing.

In the back of my mind, a small voice says that I'm lying to myself. Losing Zin simply broke me. After my sister was taken, I began playing these different characters. Family Fuck Up. Lone Vigilante. Rock Chick. Even if I wanted to share my audax obsession with anyone, I simply couldn't. The masks are me. It's not a choice anymore. It just *is*.

I tell the voice to shut up for now and I'll feed us extra popcorn later. As always, that promise works like a charm.

Straightening my spine, I focus on what's important—the Wurtzite dagger. It will be here soon. *Ah, sweet distraction.* Once I get the blade, I can go vampire hunting again.

Thump, thump, thump.

The music hits a crescendo. With each progressive beat, more frustration tightens across my shoulders. Obviously, leaning against the wall and sulking isn't doing me any favors. I need to release some anxiety.

Hello, dance floor.

6

MACK

I wait in the alley behind Club Nova. Brick buildings tower on either side of me. A band of dark sky arches overhead while a thin driveway curls beneath my feet. I check my watch.

11:04 PM

Sixty-three minutes ago, I arrived in New York with my crew, namely Ace, Zero, Jenna and Dani. By now I should be inside the club and approaching my target. I tap my earpiece, activating the com.

A voice crackles over the device. "Jessa here."

"Where are Ace and Zero?" I ask.

Those two were supposed to deliver my souped-up Wurtzite dagger by 10:45 at the latest. Nothing can start until I have the false version of that weapon.

"They left HQ ten minutes ago," says Jenna. By *HQ*,

Jenna means the fake dry cleaning van where she and Dani wait. It's parked a few blocks away from this very spot.

"Got it." I click off the com.

Damn. Ace and Zero should be here. I straighten my shoulders, waiting for frustration to burn inside me.

Nothing.

A thought appears. At some point, I won't just feel empty anymore… I'll forget I had emotions in the first place. Somehow, that'll be worse.

Finally, a silhouette appears in the mouth of the alley. *It's Ace.* He's a bulky guy who could've chosen a career in pro wrestling if vampire killing didn't pan out. Like always, Ace sports cropped gray hair, stubble along his square jawline, and a massive chip on his shoulder.

He saunters up and hands over the dagger.

"You're late," I declare.

"Got held up."

With anyone else, I'd order them back to the Fortress for being both a dick and a failure. But Ace and Roman have a special friendship. And by *special*, I mean Ace kisses Roman's ass and Roman lets him. I pick my battles.

Speaking of Ace, his gaze flickers toward the alley's entrance. "So, are we going into the club or what?"

"*I'm* going. *You're* heading back to the van."

Zero jogs into the alley. Like Jenna and Dani, Zero's in his late teens and at what we zoetic call drone level. *Barely out of training.* He's a lanky kid with long black hair, acne, and an unreasonable level of adoration for Ace.

Zero sighs. "There you are, Ace. Thought I lost you."

Ace ignores Zero and keeps all his attention on me. "Of course, I'm going into the club. I'm a paladin, same as you."

"What's wrong, buddy?" Zero elbows Ace. "Is he going all *Mako* on you?"

"Enough," I state. "I need *both* of you back in the van."

After this scene, Ace will definitely *boo hoo* to Roman that I didn't take him into the club. But at the end of the day, this mission must succeed. If that means Ace hangs in the van, it's where he goes. There's a reason Roman asks me to lead these crews in the first place. I never fail.

"What about me?" asks Zero. "I'm training to be a relic hunter. If you take me into the club, I can help you protect the weapon."

"I've got the dagger, Zero. Your part's done."

I check the blade over. It certainly looks like a real Wurtzite dagger. *No way the princess will suspect what this thing can really do.* I set the blade into a holster at the base of my spine.

"Mack is right," agrees Ace. "*Your* work is done, Zero.

I'm the spy, so I'll hit the club." He turns his steely gaze on me. "You need me to pinpoint the target, right?"

Here we go again.

"You know the situation. I lead this crew."

A muscle ticks along Ace's jawline. "You don't know the first thing about the *real* zoetic. I run everything. You should show more respect."

"And I lead this mission. Back to the van."

Somehow, Zero gets Ace to finally step away. As I watch the pair leave, I rub my neck and consider my options. In his current state of mind, Ace is a risk to himself and the crew. I'll talk to Roman later about getting Ace some leave. It won't be the first time I've asked, and so far it hasn't worked. Roman insists that Ace join every one of my missions.

Once Ace and Zero are well and really gone, I shake out my shoulders. Loosening up is part of my ritual before a gig.

Focus, Mack. Be here now.

I take in a few more deep breaths, picture my target and crack my neck.

Get the princess, find the relic, and save my people.
It's on.

7

KAPS

Where are you, Mack?

I just boogied my way through three dance tunes. Still, there's no sign of my target. Not gonna lie. My nerves are starting to fray.

Tune number four cranks up; I stifle the urge to scream. Meanwhile my tail gently pokes some chick who's invading my floor space, so that helps.

Not really.

Oh, well. I'm girl enough to admit when I need to kick a mission to the curb.

One more dance and that's it.

I'm calling Huntress.

8

MACK

On my way, Princess.

Leaving the alley, I step up to the club. The traditional brick facade is souped up by a loose grid of dark metal. A line of club goers fills the sidewalk, ending with a top-heavy guy. *The bouncer.* I slip him a hundred dollar bill and cross the threshold.

Inside, the club is the same mix of bare brick and shiny metal. Lights pulse. Music blares. I find a shadowy corner and wait. A few girls stop by and try engaging me in conversation. I give one word answers; they leave.

A dim memory appears. Time was, I'd enjoy chatting up girls in a club. Hard to imagine it now, though.

That's when I see her.

My target.

And she's dancing.

The princess wears leather shorts, a bandeau top and funky sneakers. Energy and life pulse around her.

Her eyes aren't bright; they glow with intelligence.

She doesn't just smile; she beams.

Her movements aren't only sexy; they mesmerize.

My blood heats with desire. I want to talk to her. Touch her skin. Lick her lips. Protect her beauty with everything that's in me.

It's been so long since I felt anything. *Really felt.* I simply soak in the moment for the gift it is.

For the first time in months, I'm truly alive once more.

9

KAPS

*A*t last.

I spy my target standing off to one side of the dance floor.

Mack.

He's a mountain of a guy in worn jeans and black T-shirt. Yet even without the description from Huntress, I'd know this man was a zoetic. All of them have this stoic intensity, like they're ready to slam their heads through a brick wall.

Tilting my head, I try to guess his order.

League of Bounty Hunters?

Order of Assassins?

Cabal of Ghosts?

Relic Masters?

I'll go with the last option, considering how he's got

a Wurtzite dagger and is waiting here for his buyer. Mack can't be older than nineteen, so he's probably drone level. A newbie.

And according to intel, he's got the dagger on him somewhere.

One way to find out.

I cross the room and pause before him. An electric sort of energy moves between us, making the air feel heavier.

"Hey," I say.

"Hi."

His chiseled face is far too handsome for his own good. A scar lines his chin, too. I am a sucker for someone who's been in a fight or two.

Now, I have my rules. One of them even comes from the paladin level of the zoetic.

No emotions. No entanglements.

At this point, I could pinch a nerve on this guy and drop him like a sack of potatoes. Or I could dance with him a little and try to find out where he's hiding the dagger.

One little dance won't hurt.

Gripping his hands, I steer Mack onto the dance floor. He follows my lead. I also love a big dude who doesn't mind being guided a bit. It's hot.

All of which leads to another realization. Most big

guys have the dance skills of a brick. But this one? He's got serious moves. There are things he does with his hips that get me thinking. I've been saving myself. Not sure what for, but I'll know it when I see it. Maybe it's this man.

Stop it, Kaps.

No emotions. No entanglements.

After a few songs, my thigh is between his legs and we're grinding away to the beat of yet another tune. Mack leans in and almost-not-quite kisses my neck. It's making me crazy.

Mack leans in close. His breath fans over my mouth. I inhale a scent of cinnamon and musk. My insides over-heat. Every nerve ending in my body stays attuned to his next move.

This is it. Mack is finally about to kiss me.

Only he doesn't.

Instead, Mack takes my hand and leads me off the dance floor. This would be the perfect moment to do that nerve-pinch move, but what can I say?

I'm curious what he's planning.

And yes, maybe I still want that kiss. It's all part of a mission anyway. The Lone Vigilante has pretended stuff like this before. Anything for a good magical relic.

We reach the back wall of the club. Mack presses the emergency door open. An alarm blares for a few seconds, but the sound is barely audible over the club music. We step out into the relatively cool air of a back alley. Fortunately, it's a cute space: no stinky dumpsters or pee stains on the brickwork.

Mack flips me against the wall. My bare skin presses against the rough texture of brick.

"I'm going to kiss you now," he says in a low and rumbly voice.

"Please."

Every inch of my body flares to life as he leans in.

Yes.

MACK

*U*sing my body weight, I press the princess further against the wall. Her soft curves perfectly match the rough planes of my chest. Never in my life have I felt as *complete* as I do in this moment.

I can't wait to taste her.

Leaning in, I take her mouth. Our tongues explore and slide. Fresh waves of desire pour through me. Emotions turn so intense, it's enough to make me lose track of time. I never want this to end.

It's the princess who returns to the business of the evening, namely the Wurtzite dagger.

She starts her search.

Reaching forward, the princess rubs her hands over my chest and thighs. She's nowhere near the dagger, but I don't mind how she's looking. The princess the slides her hands about my waist and that's when she hits it. The fake Wurtzite dagger is holstered at the base of my spine.

The princess nips my lower lip as she pulls the weapon free from its holster. Little by little, she circles her arm backward.

Time to act.

There's a second that lasts forever where I soak in every aspect of this woman. Intelligent eyes. Soft mouth. Gorgeous body. Sneaky as Hell personality. She's everything.

Yet she's also what prevents three hundred and four zoetic from recovering.

In the end, there's only one thing to do. I initiate the blade's spell by whispering two magic words. "Mutata nunc."

Instantly the blade melts into tiny cords that wrap around the princess' wrists. Other metal lines swoop over to her left hand and bind her there as well.

The princess frowns. "What the Hell?"

The moment shatters my heart. I'm slammed by the way the princess's brows pull together in anger. The shock in her brown eyes. And how her body stiffens with fear.

I want nothing more than to end this now. Reverse the spell. Keep the princess safe.

Yet, what I want doesn't really matter. I must save the zoetic.

Paladin training is all about control. Now I lean into my years of learning. Somehow, I'm able to keep an appearance of calm. When I next speak, my tone is all business. "Hello, Princess."

The fake dagger does its thing. The princess wobbles from side to side. To steady herself, she leans against the wall.

"Who are you?" she asks.

I'm pretty sure she's asking what my level is within the zoetic. I answer with something that's incomplete, but true.

"Name's Mack," I state. "I'm a bounty hunter."

The princess blinks at me. Clearly, she's trying to process my words, but her head's turning fuzzy. She grips my shirt, revealing the zoetic mark at the base of my neck.

"You're a paladin. Why would the zoetic send you?"

"*L'Griffe* sent me, not the zoetic. Gage doesn't like how you've been taking his magical stuff."

"Gage," slurs Kaps. The magic is really kicking in now. "That's the leader. I won't go to him. I'll fight you."

"You don't know how." The princess is badass, but it's a rare magic user who could counteract the spell in this metal.

Technically, I'm not supposed to chat up targets on a mission. But in this case, I keep talking to the princess. Maybe if she understands what happens next, things will be a little bit easier for her.

"In about ten seconds, that metal will finish reacting with the shifter magic inside you. You're about to pass out."

Her eyes flutter as she fights the need to sleep. A mixture of grief and rage fill my soul. This woman brings my heart back to life.

Why must I be forced to hurt her?

Shaking my head, I force my thoughts back to the enchanted zoetic. My friends will die unless I find the Halcyon witches and the Essence. Handing over the princess will make that happen.

Part of me points out that the princess is an amazing operative. Her file was mind-blowing. If anything, she'd make an excellent partner in my search for the serum.

Another part counters that I'll never get the Essence unless I find the Halcyons. And that means giving Gage what he wants.

The princess.

KAPS

*B*efore, my head felt a little fuzzy. Now, it's downright murky. All my muscles go into *wet noodle mode*. I squint at Mack as I fight a losing battle to stay awake.

How can he be a paladin? It doesn't add up.

Somehow, I force out some words.

"But you kissed really well," I whisper.

"So did you, Princess."

Here's the thing. Mack has these searing blue eyes that seem to say, *I'm not lying about enjoying your kisses, even though I'm dragging you away to the evil shifter mafia.*

My legs finally give way. I'm taking a one-way trip to the pavement when my world turns into darkness.

MACK

The enchanted handcuffs finish their job. The princess' eyes roll into her head as her body goes limp. In what seems like slow motion, she tumbles toward the ground. Just before the princess hits the asphalt, I scoop her into my arms.

Holding the princess drives fresh blasts of sensation. I soak in the curve of her spine as she arches against my left arm. The way her bare thighs tease against my right hand. And how her torso presses deliciously against mine. My blood heats while my soul soars.

This woman is nothing less than a goddess in my arms. I never want to let her go.

So insane.

The princess cuddles against me. I can't help but notice how her lips remain swollen from our kiss.

Craving stirs at the memory. I've shared kisses before. If anything, it felt lonely to fake an emotion that I didn't really feel. That wasn't the case with the princess. Everything between us is raw and real.

Across the alleyway, I spy folks milling about the sidewalk as they wait to enter the club. A few stare in my direction and whisper.

Best out of here, fast.

There's a reason I selected this particular club for this mission. Still holding the princess, I march along the alley to a rolling garage door. I approach.

"Mack Valtas," I say.

An access pad brightens. Light sears into my eyes as the system performs a retinal scan. Once my identity is confirmed, the garage door automatically rolls up. My Escalade waits inside, as does a lot of other stuff. This little garage isn't all that big. Still, I've packed every inch. Weapons. Canned food. Tents. It's excessive but that's my style.

With gentle movements, I set the princess onto the back bench of my SUV. With a quiet moan, she curls onto her side. Questions ricochet through my mind.

Is she comfortable? Safe? Warm?

Stepping away, I inspect the nearby shelves. Pulling down a pile of blankets, I carefully tuck them around the princess' small form. Then I add some water bottles.

And a few snack bars.

Tissues.

First aid kit.

Magazines.

Talk about your red flags.

I'm supposed to hand the princess over, not act as Escalade concierge. At last, I force myself to close the vehicle's back door and slip into driver's seat. Once there, I tap my earpiece. A familiar voice sounds in my ear.

"Jessa here."

"It's Mack. You and the others are off for the night."

"You got the target?"

"Confirmed."

I shut off earpiece, pull out my phone and dial Gage. For a few seconds, there's nothing but a low buzz of static. Then a distinctive voice echoes across the device.

"Talk to me." It's Gage, all right. His voice is all rough tones smoothed over by a French accent.

"Will you trade something else for the location of the relic? I mean, other than the princess?"

"Why? Did you fail?"

"Answer the question."

"Have I ever changed my terms, even if someone offers me twice the price?"

"No." *It was worth a try, though.*

"A king sticks to his word. If people thought I could be negotiated with, I would lose my reputation." His voice lowers. "Tell me you failed and your life is over."

"I didn't fail. I'm on my way." I don't need to say more. Gage knows what I carry with me. *The princess.*

"Good. Do not turn off your phone."

"Confirmed." No doubt, Gage will use my phone to track me. Which is fine. I couldn't have called him if I didn't agree with that approach.

Pulling out of the garage, I merge into traffic and try to focus on the flow of vehicles. It isn't easy. My thoughts keep circling back to the princess. Some part of my consciousness stays bound to hers.

How can I ever give her over to Gage?

And how would I live with myself if I didn't?

Guilt and rage swirl through me. This is bad news. I can't get more involved with the princess. My first job needs to be finding the Halcyons and that serum.

This is my chance to save a single life or many.

And I've already made my choice.

KAPS

One second, I tumble toward the asphalt, ready to pass out. The next thing I know, I stand on a landscape made entirely from waist-high clouds. Blinking hard, I wait to see if my view changes.

Nope.

All clouds, all the time.

Must be a dream.

Leaning over, I inspect my clothes. I'm still in my club outfit, including my new accessory—magical hand-cuffs. Which is odd. Normally, I wear bizarre stage costumes during my dreams. Case in point: One recent nightmare had me sporting a cape of live squirrels.

Now *that* was a dream. This is something else.

A spell? Could be.

Before me, the clouds churn and rise. White puffs solidify into the shape of a woman. I smile my face off.

Grandma Myla is here.

We grandkids call her Great M, considering how she's actually a supernatural being called the Great Scala. She's also tall and curvy with red hair and a black dragonscale tail.

"Am I dreamscaping?" asks Great M. "Is this shit working?"

All of a sudden, this strange situation makes far more sense. I've heard of dreamscaping. It's where someone with extraordinary angelic powers contacts you in your sleep.

"Kaps?"

"Great M?"

"It's me, all right." She winks. "My igni told me they could pull this off. And here we are."

Great M uses little lightning bolts of power called igni to move souls to Heaven or Hell. Like her tail, Great M's igni have a mind of their own sometimes. Seems like those igni want to chat me up right now.

Must be some pretty anxious igni.

"How are you, sweetie?" Great M goes to wrap me in an embrace, but her body goes all cloudy at the last second. "Ah, crap. I guess hugging won't happen."

"I'm just glad you're here." *Which is true.*

"You're my favorite grandkid. You know that, right?"

"Great M." I roll my eyes. "You say that to all the grandkids."

Now, this is still a serious situation. I'm in enchanted handcuffs and—no doubt—getting handed off to the dragon shifter mafia. But with Great M here? It feels like a party.

Great M focuses on my wrists. "What the Hell is that?"

"Would you believe me if I said it was part of this dream?"

"No."

I blink rapidly. "Why not?"

"First, you can't use that fake-innocent blinking-routine on me. I freaking invented it. Second, my igni say you're lying."

"Well, they might be *a little* right. I'm in the tiniest bit of trouble. But please don't say anything to my parents."

"Let me think about that." Great M taps her cheek. "No, no, no. You're my mostly-favorite grandkid. I am not looking away while you—" She winces, setting her palms against her ears. "Fuuuuuuuuuuuck! I hear you, guys. Ouch!"

I've only seen this happen a few times before. Great M's igni sometimes see the future and tell her things. It often involves lots of howling inside her brain.

"Fine! I'll do it!" Great M rolls her eyes. "Zip it already!" Little by little, she lowers her hands. "Sheesh, they are on a tear."

"What's wrong?"

"It's like this. My igni want you to find the den of the Halcyon coven. The fate of all humanity hangs in the balance."

I tilt my head. "I didn't know igni cared that much about humans."

"They don't necessarily. But if too many humans die at once, it can overload my powers. And if that happens, everyone who's been sent to their afterlife by *any* Great Scala gets a free pass to roam around. I'm talking Heaven, Hell and Purgatory all bursting open at the same time."

"That sounds bad."

"I prefer to think of it as a total shit show." She sighs. "Sorry if this is a shocker."

"It's not too awful. Someone already said I should go after the Halcyons. I just didn't have it as my top job." I glance down at the handcuffs on my wrists. "It may need to wait a little bit before I can start."

"The igni say that's fine." Great M narrows her eyes. She's still listening to the igni in her mind. "Yes. Oh. That sucks. Got it. I'll tell her."

"Tell me what?"

Great M focuses on me once more. "Here's the situation. Audax are evil vampires running around Earth. Zoetic are humans who keep them in line. But lately, most of the zoetic have fallen ill. You must ask the Halcyons for help. That way, the zoetic can keep the audax from going on a killing spree, overwhelming my powers, and blah blah blah."

While the igni are being so helpful, I decide to get some extra assistance. "Do your igni have any ideas on how to remove magical items? Let's say handcu—"

Great M sets her hands against her ears. "Argh! Sorry, Baby. The igni say we've got to go. I'll catch up with you as soon as I can."

Great M vanishes in a puff of cloud.

Okay, that was strange.

Then again, it's not like any part of this situation is normal. How many times do I wear magical handcuffs while unconscious? Adding in a dreamscape from Great M isn't that much extra.

Slam!

My eyes pop open as I find myself in the back of an SUV. Around me, there are enough snacks and supplies to feed a small army. And I still wear those damned magical handcuffs.

Slam!

A crunch sounds as something punches into one side

of the vehicle. Glancing out the window, I see a pair of Humvees on either side of this SUV. Even from this distance, I can look through the glamours of the drivers. No question about it.

We're getting run off the road by vampires.

But who are *we* in this scenario?

I scan the driver's seat, finding the familiar outline of Mack's head. So that guy's still around. My stupid heart flutters at the memory of our kiss. Which is crazy. Then again, it's not necessarily the nuttiest part of this situation. That prize definitely goes to the vampires in Humvees.

Mack weaves across the road, speeds up, slows down and generally out-drives our attackers. There's no one else in the car to watch over me.

It's escape time.

Pulling on my wrists, I work to break free from the supernatural handcuffs. Nothing happens. That's no surprise, though. Mack said some magic words when he transformed the dagger into bindings, so these cuffs are his spell. As long as Mack is conscious, he's the only one who can magically release my hands.

Another option appears.

"Huntress?" I whisper.

As a glass dragon, there are plenty of times where

Huntress has been nearby while I wasn't aware of her presence. Total invisibility bonus.

"Are you there?" I ask again.

There's no reply, but that's not a shocker. Huntress always finds her target, and since I didn't meet her at the club, she'll track me down eventually. Sometimes that can take a while. Normally, I'm happy for that fact, as it gives me time to kill more audax.

Not so today.

The car swerves from side to side. Tires screech. Another thud sounds as someone slams into our SUV again.

Any second now, we're hitting the pavement.

Only one thing left to do.

Brace for impact and await my chance to get the Hell out of here.

14

MACK

*D*amned *audax.*

Early morning sunlight gleams off the hood of my Escalade as I speed down a remote Vermont road. Grasslands stretch off in every direction. There's nothing around but a few cows.

Oh, and two Humvees filled with vampires.

As I speed along, my SUV is sandwiched between two military-grade Humvees. All three vehicles tool along at a healthy hundred-plus miles an hour.

I glance from left to right. The Humvee drivers look like human military, but I can see through their glamour.

Audax.

Every so often, one of the Humvees swerves and slams into my vehicle. I speed up, slow down and veer in the opposite direction... whatever it takes to stay on the road.

Still, I can't keep this up forever.

What I wouldn't give for a senior crew at this moment. As it is, I can't regret that Jessa, Dani, Ace and Zero are miles away from here. They're not up for a high speed chase. Their van would have toppled ages ago.

A chill crawls up my back. The princess. *I can't lose her.*

"Princess?" I call. "Are you up?"

No reply. Worry twists up my spine.

"Not sure if you can hear me," I continue. "But keep your belt buckled and the blankets around you. Things might get tricky."

Slam!

The right-hand Humvee careens into my Escalade. My grip on the wheel slips, and that's a disaster.

What happens next takes place in a matter of seconds. Even so, it feels like years crawl by. The Humvee to my left slams on the brakes. The one on my right keeps plowing into the side of my vehicle.

My Escalade rolls off the road. Gravel flies against the windshield. A low boom sounds as a tire gives out. Weightlessness takes over my body as I spin through the air.

Crash!

My vehicle lands on the roof with bone-jarring impact. The SUV slides along for a few yards, taking down overgrown grass as it goes. I hang upside down by the seat belt. Blood drips from my nose and fingertips. Gravel crunches as the Humvees pull to a stop. Voices sound as at least three audax march toward my position.

White stars blur my vision. My body turns numb.

Whatever happens, I can't pass out.

Not sure I'll have much of a choice.

15

KAPS

So the SUV just rolled.

Meh.

With all my strength, I kick through the side window and crawl out from the wreck. I'm vaguely aware of noises and bodies nearby. All my focus narrows to two goals.

One, shift into my dragon form.

Two, fly the Hell away.

Only trouble is, these stupid handcuffs block my shifting powers. I yank at my wrists. The transformed dagger holds firm.

Then it changes.

Suddenly, the cuffs on my wrists morph back to a Wurtzite dagger. The blade drops onto the grass, harmless. I pause, confused.

Why did the spell end?

With quiet steps, I move around to the front of the SUV. There, three figures yank a very bloody Mack out the driver's side window of the upside-down Escalade. All of them are vampires wearing army fatigues, as if they're part of the human military.

A glitter of light surrounds one of the audax as he transforms from a man in camouflage into a skeletal figure wearing a tattered Nazi uniform. Chunks of skin have fallen off his frame, exposing the decaying veins and muscles.

The rotting audax kneels beside Mack.

No, no, no.

The vampire pulls back Mack's T-shirt. I've seen this move before. The blood sucker is going in for the kill.

Every cell in body seems to freeze. All thoughts of flying to safety simply vanish.

I stood by once while my sister Zin was taken from me. No way I'll let that happen again.

Kneeling, I grab the fake dagger from the ground and eye the blade. Perhaps I can use this to stop the audax. Unfortunately, the weapon now has the strength of cardboard.

Not helpful.

My mind spins through more options. If I can take

down an audax with nothing but my tail and a turtle, I can figure out something here.

That's when it happens.

The vampire latches onto Mack's throat.

Rage spikes through me, more intense than anything I've ever felt before.

Simply put, I lose my mind.

And by this I mean, my dragon takes over.

What happens next is total instinct. My clothes burst off as I transform into my dragon self: a wiry beast of black and violet. Leaning back on my haunches, I let out a massive roar.

Then I leap in and attack.

16

MACK

*M*y head feels fuzzy, like my skull got stuffed with rags. Pain radiates through my limbs. My ears ring with a high-pitched tone.

What's happening again?

Oh, yeah. I got run off the road by audax.

Little by little, I force my eyes to open. I expect to find myself back inside my car, only upside down.

That's not the case.

Instead of being in my car, I'm flat on my back in an open field. A few points on my throat sting with pain. It's a telltale sign an audax tried to bite me and failed. Not the first mission where that has happened. Won't be the last, either. Usually, I beat the bloodsuckers off before they get too far.

Only this time, I was unconscious during the attack.

I frown. It isn't like an audax to back off a meal.

Roar!

Something lets out a mighty bellow. The noise is loud enough to fully awaken me. I turn my head, curious what's going on.

What I see is a stunner.

A great black dragon battles nearby. A crown of violet horns encircles its head. More purple spikes jut up from its long tail.

There can only be one explanation.

This is Princess Kaps.

My one-time captive has transformed in her dragon self, and she's kicking some serious audax ass.

Dragon-Kaps tears, bites and stomps. All the vampires still look like military folks. More of them must have left their Humvees in order to join the battle. Now there are about a dozen audax in all. Some climb up Dragon-Kaps' back. Others jab her with cattle prods. Even more hack at her hide with swords.

None are making a dent.

Dragon-Kaps tears off vampire heads and spits the skulls aside. She slices through more with her talons. Others she simply stomps into the ground.

This isn't killing them, though. The only way to fully end an audax is to plunge a golden stake through their heart. Otherwise they can—and will—reform and cause trouble.

Deep inside me, something awakens. Jolts of rage move through my limbs. A single thought absorbs my consciousness: *Kaps is threatened.* Until those audax are truly dead, they could hurt her.

Blood still drips down my face. Pain pulses through my limbs. Pushing past the agony, I force myself to stand. I always keep a golden stake strapped to my calf. Now I pull out the weapon and stagger toward the battle.

Seeking out each downed audax, I stake them right through the heart. After every strike, a golden light surrounds the vampire. My target then transforms from a warrior in modern fatigues into a very decayed corpse in an old Nazi uniform. A second round of golden brightness follows. When this light fades, the audax body is gone, replaced by a heap of ash. Or in some cases, multiple small piles.

Dragon-Kaps and I work in tandem. She downs the audax, I stake each one. There's no need to talk and set up a plan. The movements simply happen. Soon, all the audax are dead and—just as importantly—vanished.

Baring her teeth, Dragon-Kaps scans the rolling fields around us. There's nothing around but the overturned Escalade and two Hummers. Her eyes flare with violet light.

I suppose I should be uneasy. After all, I've never been this close to a dragon before. Sure, I've seen them wing across the sky while other humans couldn't detect anything. But it's one thing to pick out a small figure speeding through a cloud and having a living dragon the size of an eighteen-wheeler loom before me.

And the sight feels natural. Which is supremely strange.

Dragon-Kaps swings her mighty head in my direction. Her chest heaves in heavy breaths.

Striding closer, I carefully inspect her dragon scales. None seem to be dented, let alone hurt. Still, you never know when a small injury can cause big trouble.

"Are you all right?" I ask.

Purple light surrounds Dragon-Kaps. One moment, a massive dragon towers beside me. The next second, my view has changed.

To a very naked Kaps.

And she stands only a few inches away.

I'm definitely attracted to this girl—our kiss at the dance club proved that—but there are more important things to focus on right now.

"Are you all right?" I ask again.

Kaps shakes her head. "What about you?" She glances at my throat. "They were attacking you."

"Barely broke the skin."

She brushes her fingertips along my hairline. "What about your head? There's so much blood."

"I'm a quick healer. I'll be fine." I gently clasp her wrist. "Thank you."

A pretty shade of pink colors Kaps' face. "It was my dragon. She can't stand to see the audax attack anyone."

"My appreciation to her as well. She's beautiful."

"I lost control back there." Kaps' blush deepens. "Normally, I bring a change of clothes."

It takes a moment for me to process her words. Before, I'd been too concerned that Kaps was injured. Now I become incredibly aware of Kaps' naked body. Again.

I ache to run my fingertips down her throat and explore more of her skin. But that won't happen. Kaps ended up unclothed because she shifted in order to protect me. I won't do anything that could take advantage.

Still, there's no avoiding the fact that I've spent years learning how to detect things in my peripheral vision. I don't need to stare to know how gorgeous she is.

Lowering my hand, I pull on my neckline. "You want my shirt?"

Kaps nods.

I pull off my T and hand it over. To me, this shirt is snug. On Kaps, it dangles down to her knees. Deep inside me, some part of me is pleased that Kaps wears something with my scent.

My mind takes a snapshot of this moment. Over the last few minutes, I was bitten by a vampire, fought beside a dragon, and staked some audax.

Yet all of that pales compared to the most critical fact.

Kaps fought for me.

Something deep in my soul shifts again, only more forcefully this time. Fresh cords of connection wind between us. This girl should have run the first moment she was free, and yet she stayed and saved my life.

That means everything.

17

KAPS

A second ago, I was naked. Normally, that's no big deal for a dragon shifter. Our kind end up clothes-free all the time. But with Mack around? Talk about awkward.

Now, Mack stands before me and he's naked from the waist up.

I ache to reach out and set my palm against his chest. Which brings up a good idea. While I'm touching Mack's chest, I could check out his backside as well. I missed that opportunity when we were kissing outside the club. After all, I'm still on a mission. None of this is real.

Then it hits me. Maybe Mack is waiting for me to make the first move.

Our gazes lock. There's fire in those ice-blue eyes.

Oh, he's definitely waiting for me.

In fact, I'm about to reach forward and start the fun times when Mack breaks up the moment.

"The L'Griffe are still after you," says Mack.

"I'm aware."

"No, I mean they're pulling up right now."

Turning, I see a line of three stretch Bentleys tooling toward us. There's no mistaking the knife pattern in the grille of each vehicle. That's L'Griffe, all right.

"You want to fly away?" asks Mack. "I can stall them."

"You'd seriously do that for me?"

His gaze turns even more intense. "You saved my life. I have promises to keep, but I owe you."

I frown. "Promises to keep? Will something happen to you if I'm not taken?"

"Not me, others."

A memory appears. In my dreamscape with Great M, she said something about the zoetic being sick. That's why the igni want me to hunt down the Halcyon coven in the first place. Maybe that's what Mack is working toward, as well.

I straighten my shoulders. "Well, I appreciate the offer, but I won't run from the L'Griffe. They fly, same as I do."

"Good point." He lowers his voice. "We'll figure this out, Kaps."

I like his confidence, but if my calculations are correct, there will be more than a dozen dragon shifters against me and Mack.

Not great odds.

18

MACK

The stretch Bentleys pull over to the side of the road. Gage Beaumont steps out from the first one. Like all L'Griffe, he's a picture-perfect guy, what with his trim frame, dark hair and Armani suit. As always, his blue tail sways behind him in a predatory rhythm.

I nod in Gage's direction. "Hey."

"I received reports of audax activity in zee area," says Gage. "Thought I might meet you half way."

The L'Griffe HQ lies inside Quebec's Mount Valin, so this place is indeed the midpoint between Manhattan and the mountain.

Gage steps around to the front of his Bentley. Leaning back, he half sits, half leans on the vehicle's hood. Which I guess you can do when you're king. Gage raises his hand, palm upward, and flaps his fingers in a way that says, *bring her here.*

I don't move. Neither does Kaps.

Going back on a deal with the L'Griffe is serious business. Roman could kick me out of the zoetic. If that happens, I can't help Ndidi and the others.

Damn.

A dividing line opens in my life. On one side, there's being in the zoetic. Following the rules. Protecting my comrades. But on the other side, there's Kaps. Just looking at her fills my soul with devotion.

Before the audax attack, I'd have chosen the zoetic every time. But Kaps brought back my heart and saved my life. I simply can't send her off to an execution.

There must be another way to find the Halcyons. Assuming I live past this encounter, that is.

"Hand over the princess," orders Gage.

I move to stand between Kaps and the L'Griffe. "Let's talk about this."

Gage frowns. "Can Mack, the great Mako, be getting soft-hearted for a girl? She is not worth it."

"What do you want?" I ask. "There must be something."

"I desire one thing," counters Gage. "Princess Kaps.

You know I never change terms on a deal." He glares at me, his eyes glowing red with demonic power and anger.

This isn't going well.

19

KAPS

*D*ang, *Gage really hates my guts.*

I'd never taken the L'Griffe seriously before. Maybe it's the dressy clothes or the froufrou accent. Plus, the L'Griffe are dragon shifters, so I figured there was the *princess factor* working in my favor. But now? Looks like I misjudged how much I bothered Gage. All of which raises a nasty question.

What do the L'Griffe want to do with me?

I'm guessing it's not a fun sleepover where we braid each other's hair and tell ghost stories.

Gage snaps his fingers. More L'Griffe henchmodels pour out of their stretch Bentleys. Sixteen in total. That's a tough number to fight, considering all those L'Griffe guys can change into dragons.

Suddenly, I hear another familiar noise, namely the flapping of invisible wings.

There's a particular sound that dragons make when they fly. After a while, you can learn their rhythm like humans record fingerprints. Which is why I know exactly who's about to land.

Huntress. Her wings are insect-style and mimic dragonflies. There's no missing that distinct buzz.

The L'Griffe hear it, too. Everyone pauses as they wait for the newcomer to appear, which is wise. Never attack an unknown dragon.

"Do you hear that?" I ask.

Mack nods. "One of yours?"

"My sister Huntress. I was supposed to meet her at the club last night. She's worried."

"About you?"

"Sure."

Mack looks genuinely shocked. "But our files have you as a paladin-level operative. You can take care of yourself and then some."

And does that revelation make me a wee bit happy? Oh, yes.

"About that," I state. "My family doesn't know I hunt audax. I'd like to keep it that way."

Mack narrows his eyes. "Let me get this straight.

Your family seriously thinks you're a rock chick who chases down relics."

Clearly, Mack finds this hard to believe. Having grown up where everyone thinks I'm a loser means one thing. *This is my favorite conversation ever.*

I shrug. "It's a long story but yeah, that's how it is."

Suddenly, a familiar beat of wings fills the air, only far louder this time. Huntress appears. I must say, my sister looks fearsome in her leather fighting suit. Purple, naturally. That's Huntress' color.

A side note on Huntress. Glass dragons don't end up naked unless they want to. Their whole body is liquid, so Huntress creates her own outfits on the fly. Mostly, she sports purple leather.

Huntress strides to stand between me and Gage. She's so badass, it isn't even funny. A long pause follows while all the L'Griffe shifters merely stare at my sister.

I don't blame them, either. Huntress is impressive. And since she's the last glass dragon, everyone always watches her in awe. Until she starts fighting. Then their gazes change into looks of pure terror.

It's Gage who breaks up the moment.

By laughing.

"And zees," he says in his Frenchy accent. "Zees is supposed to be a glass dragon?"

That ticks me off. "Hey, my sister *is the* last glass dragon. Show some respect."

Gage shakes his head. "Do you know how easy it is to cast spells that replicate zee glass dragon effect?"

At these words, Huntress turns all transparent-like and stalks over to Gage. I love this look; it's as if she's made from water. Fast as a whip, Huntress retakes her full-color form while setting her dagger against Gage's throat.

"My sister doesn't lie," states Huntress.

At this point, I could share that I pretty much fib all the time, but this is Huntress' moment. She'll start kicking ass any second now.

Only she doesn't.

Instead of beating each other up, Huntress and Gage share the mother of all eye-locks. Gage inhales deeply. I'm talking about his nostrils flaring and everything.

So that's happening. Sniffing.

Next Huntress does something I never expected. She leans forward and starts kissing Gage. On the mouth. And with tongue action.

I blink hard, not believing what I'm seeing.

Yet no matter how much I try to clear my eyes, it's still there.

Huntress is making out with Gage.

For the record, my sister isn't the kissy type. I mean,

Zin and I talk about the smoochy side of life, but Huntress shows zero interest. In fact, I'm pretty sure this might be her first kiss, ever.

Whoa.

It gets pretty hot, too. I decide that now is a great time to stare at the grass. *Hey, that stuff is green.* And there's a broken old sign for Benjamin's Dairy Farm nearby. So cows used to eat here.

Wow.

Trivia.

Okay. She's got to be done by now.

I sneak a look.

Nope.

The kissing continues. And Huntress' blade remains pressed against Gage's throat the entire time. All the L'Griffe guys gaze upon the scene. Their handsome faces are the very definition of *longing.*

Things just keep getting weirder and weirder.

I need something else to focus on, so I look over to Mack. That's worse. It just reminds me how he tasted last night.

At last, Huntress breaks away from Gage.

"Um, guys?" I ask.

No reply. It's like I don't exist.

"Is this dagger for me?" The way Gage asks this question, he could be asking if Huntress means to kill him.

But I doubt it. There's way too much sexual tension in the air. Plus, I get the distinct feeling there are layers at work here that I don't understand.

Maybe my sister doesn't, either.

"Don't answer that question, Huntress," I warn.

If Huntress hears me, she doesn't show it. Instead, my sister brushes a gentle kiss against Gage's lips. "Yes, the dagger is yours."

"Thank you," says Gage. "All contracts against your sister Kaps are null and void."

So I'm out of trouble.

Wait, what?

Don't get me wrong. I'm happy that there's no longer a contract on my head. But I still have this creepy sensation that things are going on which I don't understand. More importantly, neither does Huntress.

Gage looks to Mack. "Midnight. Tomorrow night. Devil's Park, New York. We L'Griffe have a cabin by the cliff wall. What you seek lies in there."

"Thank you," says Mack.

Now, I haven't been chasing down relics all my life not to know treasure-map style instructions when I hear them. Color me interested.

Gage brushes his finger along Huntress' jawline. "Au revoir, mon ange."

Huntress shivers. The movement seems to snap her

out of some kind of trance. She wheels around to focus on me. "Are you all right, Kaps?"

That's classic Huntress. Always worrying about other people.

"I'm fine. What about you?"

"You must return home immediately," announces Huntress. "Mum and Da have been trying to reach you for hours."

Now, I can't help but notice how Huntress ignored the whole *what about you* question. That said, I know my sister. Whatever's happening, she won't blab in front of Gage and his henchmodels.

So I change the subject.

"I'm headed back to the tower, aren't I?"

"Something like that." Huntress twiddles her fingers, a hand sign that means magic will be involved. When it comes to my home land of Furonium, I can sneak out of almost any situation, expect when spells are in the mix. Still, that's my problem. Huntress has enough to worry about.

"Thanks for coming after me."

Normally, this is where we share a joke or two. Huntress says something like, *she has nothing else to do but chase after my dumb butt.* Then I distract her from figuring out that I just killed some vampires. It's good stuff. Yet not this time.

"I'll see you back at the palace," says Huntress. With that, my sister vanishes. There's the tell tale beating of wings as she transforms into her dragon self and takes to the skies.

My insides twist with worry. Huntress and I always fly home together. Things keep getting more odd. How good of a kisser can Gage be, really? Maybe Huntress is just too sheltered.

For his part, Gage opens his suit coat to expose an empty dagger holster. *That's what you call suspicious with a capital S.* Gage sets Huntress' dagger into the holster and saunters back into his ride. Within a minute, all three stretch Bentleys are tooling down the road in the opposite direction.

Mack and I are alone again.

20

MACK

The L'Griffe are gone.

So is Huntress.

Little by little, Kaps turns to face me once more. I can't help but notice how right she looks in my T-shirt. Part of me wants to pull her into my arms. More of me knows that it's best if we both move on with our lives as quickly as possible. Less pain all around. I'm a cursed human surrounded by a dying legion of zoetic. That's not who Kaps deserves.

"How will you get home?" she asks.

"Once the SUV flipped, it sent out an alert. My ride will be here soon."

"Ah. Friendlies."

"That's right."

Zoetic rely on humans to help us out. *The Friendlies.*

Most have a little demon DNA, same as I do. Only unlike the zoetic, these humans don't want to get involved. Time was, I thought that being zoetic made me a better person. But after what happened just now? I'm not so sure.

I step closer to Kaps. "I want you to know something. I would never have taken this mission if I had any other choice. I don't kidnap girls."

Kaps' tail waves to me over her shoulder. "Don't get too high on your own juice, Bud. It's not like I'm a regular girl here. I would have escaped eventually."

A sense of pride warms my chest. Not many operatives can get the best me. Kaps is definitely one of them.

"I'm still sorry. I don't know what else to say."

Kaps meets my gaze for a long time. I can almost picture the wheels of her mind turning. Only unlike Ace, I don't get a seedy vibe about it.

At last, Kaps speaks again. "Look, I get it. I know the other zoetic are sick. By handing me over to the L'Griffe, you would have helped them somehow. Am I right?"

"I should've guessed you'd figure it out. Yes, that's exactly what I was doing. And my work isn't over, either. My next stop is finding the Halcyon coven. They may have a healing serum that can fix things."

"I've been wanting to meet that coven, too. Gage

gave you instructions for finding a relic to locate the Halcyons, am I right?"

"Yes. Are you saying we should team up?"

This could be perfect. If I have Kaps along on a mission to the Halcyon coven, then my chances of success are much better. And some deep part of me loves the idea of keeping her close and safe.

Kaps sighs. "It's like this. When I'm on a mission, I can fool around to get a relic or whatever. But other than that, I work alone. It's always been that way for me."

The air between turns heavy with sorrow. "I respect that." *And I do.*

"Guess I better go." Kaps scans the skies. "My easiest path back to Furonium is to wing it." She pulls on neckline of my shirt. "You want it back?"

"No, it's yours."

Purple light surrounds Kaps as she transforms into a dragon. My shirt lies in tatters on the ground, and somehow that's a fitting sight.

She really is a beautiful dragon.

How I hate watching her fly away.

21

KAPS

*a*s I wing off, I know I should keep my focus on the clouds. After all, one of these puffballs is actually a magical portal back to my home world of Furonium.

Still, I can't help myself.

All I want is one little peek.

Flipping over, I fly backwards and check out Mack. He's now a small point on a vast sea of green. The sight makes my heart crack.

I panicked when Mack asked about teaming up. No one even knows about my Lone Vigilante side, let alone works with that person. And don't get me started on how Mack also knows I'm a princess. I can't let the different versions of me get all mixed together.

In the end, it's probably best that Mack and I never

see each other again. Mack is human. I'll live for thousands of years. There's no way our relationship would end in anything but agony.

So I force myself to turn away and wing toward the clouds.

And I don't look back again.

22

MACK

Soon after Kaps leaves, a Friendly picks me up and takes me to JFK. Once I'm at the airport, I hop on the first flight to Florida. From there, yet another Friendly gives me a ride to the Zoetic Fortress.

It's not that I have anything against regular humans, by the way. It's just that Friendlies can actually see the supernatural. And that's useful, particularly when you're finding your way to the Fortress. The place is coated with glamour spells that hide it from the general public.

It's not long before my Friendly driver tools up to a tall gray castle that towers over an abandoned beach. *The Fortress.* As I hand over a pile of cash and step out of the car, I cling to my last memories of Kaps.

Her magnetic smile.

The soothing alto of her voice.

And the press of her mouth against mine.

With each passing moment, those recollections fade. Emptiness creeps into my soul once more. After being with Kaps, it's like entering a room filled with smoke after breathing fresh air.

Forget her, Mack.

As the Friendly drives away, I march up the main steps to the Fortress. Pressing open the front door, I step into the main entrance chamber. It's a tall stone space with arched ceilings. Pendants from the different orders line the walls. A thin stream of zoetic march through the various archways.

I'm about to head under the arch for the healing chamber when I notice it.

Jenna and Zero talking in a corner.

Although talk isn't really the right word here. It's more of a verbal battle. Jenna's face is fierce as thunder. Zero's brows are pulled together in the classic look that says, *what did I do?*

I've known Zero and Jenna have been dating. So long as it doesn't interfere with their work, the zoetic allow it. But I've never seen either of them this upset.

Someone else thinks the same as I do. *Ace.* He stands under the archway that leads to the healing chamber, and he's watching Jenna and Zero with a level of interest that definitely falls in the zone of creepy.

I march over to his side. "Move along, Ace. Jenna and Zero deserve their privacy."

Ace sniffs. "If they wanted to be subtle, they should have chatted on the beach."

"That wasn't a request."

"We're not a mission. You don't order me around." He grins. "Although I'll get to that to *you* today. Roman wants you in the laboratory."

I glance down the hallway toward the healing chamber. "I was on my way to visit Ndidi."

"Not now." Ace chuckles.

The guy really is a dick.

Ace makes *shoo fingers* at me. "Off to the lab, little rat." As he says those words, there's a particular gleam in Ace's eyes that I don't like at all. And the way Ace glances toward the healing chamber? I like that even less.

What is Ace really up to? Does he just talk a good game about running the zoetic... or is he really pulling strings behind the scenes?

I take off for the archway that leads to Roman and with any luck, some answers.

23

KAPS

Home sweet dragon lands.

After a long flight back, I return to my family's palace in Furonium. After a quick change, I now stand in the waiting room for my parents' audience chamber. It's a large space made of red granite. A pair of tall black doors line one wall, along with a set of Kathikon guards in black suits and bowler hats. I've run across these two particular chicks before. Everyone calls them Gamma and Slamma. It's Slamma who whispers in my direction.

"Hey, PUP."

PUP stands for Pretty Useless Princess. Funny, eh? I never thought so, either. And I've been hearing this joke since age nine.

"What did you say?" I ask.

Both guards take care to look extra-innocent. "Nothing," says Slamma.

I pace a slow line across the floor, taking care to make my Doc Martins squeak with every step. It kills some time and irritates Slamma in particular.

"Do you need to change shoes?" asks Slamma.

"No." I pull up the velvet hem of my long sheath-dress. "Versaci recommends wearing Doc Martins with this particular gown."

Voices echo through the closed door. Eavesdropping is inevitable.

Turns out, Cerys is in the chamber right now, complaining to my parents. She's the Mistress Dragon for the Hexenwing tribe. Turns out, Cerys is none too happy that some nearby dragons—namely the very sketchy Thorntail tribe—ate all the Hexenwing cows.

That's what you call a big deal.

For dragons, cows are a delicacy as well as a pain in the ass to haul in from Earth. My parents spend a crazy amount of time on bovine fights.

At last, the double doors swing open. Mistress Cerys steps through, her chin high. She's a towering woman in black robes whose headdress is a cascade of dark feathers. Behind her shleps Master Marco from the Thorntail tribe, his shoulders slumped. Clearly, Marco will soon be flying to Earth to pick up some replacement cows.

Serves him right.

I'd high-five Mistress Cerys, but both her and Master Marco step by me as if I weren't there. A small troop of dragons in their human form follow behind—those are the Hexenwing and Thorntail courts. Most members follow the example of their leaders and ignore me. A few younger members look my way and snicker.

Yeah, I know. I'm the screw up. Ha ha.

A memory appears. Mack said that I'd qualify as a paladin. He never looked past me like I didn't exist. The realization makes bands of sorrow tighten across my chest. I shake my head, as if I can force thoughts of him from my mind.

Mack is gone. Best to adjust.

Finally, the procession ends.

"You may enter," say Gamma and Slamma in unison.

I nod.

Time to face the Imperials.

24

MACK

J find Roman in his laboratory, as always. It's a human style room with lots of white walls, long tables and shiny gadgets. Half the room is lined with walk-in refrigerators that are packed with bags of blood samples, both from the audax and their victims. Roman works constantly to figure out what's wrong with audax blood.

Or he used to.

Now most of the refrigerators are empty. All the zoetic researchers have run off or gotten enchanted by the bloom.

The thought should bother me, yet it doesn't. My heart feels hollow once more. No emotion at all. In fact, I can't even remember what it felt like to desire Kaps.

Focus on the mission, Mack. Find the Halcyons. Get the serum. Save the zoetic.

I find Roman sitting at a white counter, peering through his microscope. He doesn't look up as I approach. "Gage phoned. The king says the mission was fulfilled and all debts are paid. How did the new crew work out?"

"They stayed in the van most of the time. Ace is on edge. The guy needs a break, Roman."

"Anything else?"

"Jessa is a natural leader."

At last, Roman turns away from the microscope. "What about the princess?" His flinty gaze scans me from head to toe. I've seen that particular look before. Clearly, Gage already told Roman what happened in Vermont.

"I refused to hand Kaps over."

"And why was that?"

"The princess saved me from some audax."

Roman steeples his fingers beneath his chin. "Perhaps you deserved to die. You were sloppy to leave your crew behind."

I would disagree, but then Roman would see it as a big red arrow pointing to Kaps' head and saying, *problem.*

"Dragon shifters are dangerous," continues Roman.

"And not just because they have talons. They're masters of lust and wrath. Be on your guard. No emotions. No entanglements. Don't let feelings cloud your thinking again. Remember the inner paladin." He thumps his chest with his fist. "That's what matters."

"Yes, my Liege."

"Gage also mentioned that he gave you a lead on finding the Halcyons."

"He did."

"Good work." Roman smiles. "Keep it up."

"According to the directions from Gage, I must plan a new mission for tomorrow night."

"Ace will accompany you."

It's an effort not to groan. "As you command. If you'll excuse me."

Nodding, Roman returns his focus to his microscope. I march off to design plans and alert my crew. Jenna, Zero, Dani and Ace will accompany me again. Sad to say, they're the best the zoetic has to offer right now.

But first, there's more important work to be done.

It's beyond time to check on Ndidi.

25

KAPS

Here we go. The Family Fuck Up strikes again.

Steeling my shoulders, I march inside the imperial reception chamber.

This must be how human teenagers feel when they're called to the principal's office. Only in my case, replace the principal with two dragons.

No matter how many times I come in here, the chamber strikes me as majestic, what with its pointy ceilings and a velvet runner on the floor. Red granite is everywhere, except for the stained glass windows of dragons that line the walls.

At the far end of the chamber, my parents sit atop a pair of red wooden thrones. Mum looks ethereal with her petite frame and long blonde hair. To me, she's always seemed more like an elf queen than a dragon.

Beside her, Da strikes an imposing figure, what with his broad shoulders and loose black hair.

And they're holding hands.

That simple act reminds me that my parents are rhanas, which is what dragons call life mates. Rhanas are two shifters who are perfectly suited for each other. An emptiness fills my heart. It's rare for any dragon to find their rhana. Zin found hers as a kid. My mind circles back to Mack again.

Too bad he's human.

As I march down the central aisle toward the thrones, Huntress appears beside me. I shoot her a sly look. "Hey."

My sister nods but doesn't meet my gaze. Clearly, someone hasn't recovered from her close encounter with Gage Beaumont.

We pause at the base of the stairs leading to the thrones. No one else waits in the reception chamber. That's what you call a red flag. Plus, Mum and Da aren't coming down to hug or say hello. That's what you call *a whole ton* of red flags.

I am so getting locked in a tower.

Huntress launches right into business. "Kaps is here, as promised. Now I'm going on a retreat."

Mum leans forward. "Oh?"

Huntress shrugs. The movement is meant to look

casual, but it's clear that something is seriously bothering her. "You've been pushing me to go for a while. I need a break."

"Of course, lamb." Da's British accent makes everything sound better.

Huntress strides from the chamber, taking care to slam the doors behind her. That's another non-Huntress move.

Mum frowns. "What's wrong with Huntress?"

No point lying here. My parents won't believe the truth anyway.

"It's like this," I explain. "Huntress made out with Gage Beaufort, leader of the L'Griffe crime syndicate. She's adjusting."

A long pause follows. Then Mum and Da laugh their asses off. *Did I call it or what?*

Mum pats under her eyes. "That was funny, Kaps."

I bob my brows. "Glad I amuse."

"Let's get to it," says Mum. "You went on another mission on Earth for, uh, trinkets?"

Da elbows her. "Artifacts, luv."

"That's right," I confirm. "I was looking for a Wurtzite dagger."

"But Zinnia is safe now," says Da. "And we have many daggers in the royal treasure hoard."

"You know me," I counter. "It's all about the fun of the chase."

Normally, those words don't sting as much as they do right now. For the first time in ages, I want to yell the truth.

I hunt audax!

Mack called me a badass!

I even keep a secret lair under the palace with all my magical stuff!

But I don't say a word. I'm in enough trouble without confessing anything extra. And even if I weren't about to get locked up, there will always be parts of my life that I simply can't share. Like the Lone Vigilante.

Mum twists her hands at her waistline. "I cast a divination spell."

It takes everything in me not to gasp and step backward. Mum's a powerful magic user. "What did you see?"

"My visions are always hard to interpret," explains Mum. "This one could have been about your recent trip to Earth. According to what I witnessed, you aren't looking for relics at all. You're obsessed with hunting…" She shakes her head. "This is so silly."

"Go on," urges Da.

"I saw that you're hunting audax. I guess they are vampires."

I'm tempted to correct her that audax are actually shape-shifting vampire Nazis, but again, I hold back.

Mum sighs. "I also saw that you wish to protect humans, which is completely ridiculous."

"Humans." Da chuckles. "Even your Grandma Myla is immune to those creatures. Your grandmother processes human souls for Purgatory, but she rarely gets involved with how they reach the spiritual plane in the first place."

I shrug. "No one like humans." The words stick in my throat.

Mack is human. I like him.

"Now, we all know you have a wild streak," offers Mum.

"Hey, I had one myself," adds Da. "Travel to Earth. Have a little fun. It's all the *bee's knees*, as we say."

My parents pause and look to me. That's my cue to say something comforting.

"You have nothing to worry about," I announce.

Which is true. That said, I'm not promising to avoid Earth in the future.

"We've gotten word about someone wanting to capture you," says Da. "It's very upsetting."

Mum exhales. "We lost Zin for years, you can understand why we're protective."

I do understand. When Zin was stolen away, all of us

were devastated. In my case, my heart became permanently shattered, splitting me into my Lone Vigilante, Family Fuck Up and Rock Chick selves. For their parts, my parents became professional worriers.

Behind us, the door opens again.

"Hey, guys!"

The voice is unmistakable. Great M is here. Some of my sorrow vanishes.

"Sorry I'm late." Great M wraps me in a big hug. Leaning in, she whispers in my ear. "You're my favorite, Kaps."

I crack a smile. This is part of our regular greeting. "You say that to all of us grandkids." Our tails share a high five.

Great M gives me the side eye. "You don't say." She rounds on my parents. "Hey, Cha Cha. T."

"Good to see you." Mum's tone stays decidedly icy. That means that whatever the bad news is, my parents have yet to give it.

"We're pleased you're here," says Da. "But why the rush to join us?"

"Here's the situation," says Great M. "My igni have been blabbing in my mind non-stop."

"What do they say?" asks Mum.

"Nothing good," says Great M. "A great threat has

arisen. Kaps must visit Earth and find the Halcyon coven."

Mum and Da share a long look. Da is the one who speaks next. "We've gotten word from our spy network. Someone on Earth wishes to abduct Kaps."

"I may have heard that, too," I state. "It could even be a dragon shifter named Gage Beaumont. But there is nothing to worry about on that score. If Huntress were here, she would vouch for me."

"It doesn't matter what Huntress says," announces Mum. "You're staying here and safe. We're magically sealing off Furonium for at least a decade. That will give the humans time to stew in their own evil juices. Leave our family alone."

My shoulders slump. "A decade?"

"Consider yourself lucky it's not a century," adds Da. No doubt, he lobbied to get the number down.

I clasp my hands at my waistline. This is a long shot, but I have to try. "Please let me find the Halcyons. It's important. I'll return really quickly."

"My igni agree," says Great M. "Kaps must find these witches in their den. It's very serious. Every soul in the after-realms could be set loose."

"I agree about the importance of this situation," says Mum. Her mouth thins to a determined line.

My heart sinks. *Here it comes.*

Mum lowers her head. I can barely see her lips move, but there's no question what's up.

Mum's whispering an incantation.

A haze of red sparkles materialize around Mum's head. Her voice grows louder as she continues her spell. I can't understand a word of it, but there are tons of consonants, so it all sounds pretty badass. The sparkles congeal into a web of lines that criss-cross the room.

Mum raises her arms.

The misty red lines speed through the windows and into the ground. Pressure builds inside my temples. I can sense the bindings moving all across Furonium, sealing every last being to this realm.

My headache turns searingly painful as the red cords glow more brightly than ever before. Then the web vanishes. A dull ache still pulses behind my eyes.

It is done. I'm trapped.

Mum lowers her arms. "My *aegis web* spell just sealed off Furonium. You won't be limited to living in the tower, but you cannot leave the realm. No one can."

"Our decision is final," says Da.

I hug my elbows. "Sure. I get it."

And I do. But Great M's igni think I must find the Halycons' den. I'm on the same page as well. Long story short, there must be a way around this aegis web.

I'll just have to find it.

26

MACK

*L*eaving Roman behind, I head straight for the healing chamber. The cots are still filled with my comrades. If anything, their bodies seem to be covered in a deeper shades of red haze.

They're all getting worse.

Low moans fill the air now. Some Zoetic writhe on their beds. Others grit their teeth in agony. This is the way of the bloom: the more the pain, the closer you are to death.

I'm running out of time.

I spot Felix standing in a far corner, chatting away with Ace. The medic wears the same starry-eyed look that Zero does when conversing with the only other paladin around. For his part, Ace waves his hands as he gives yet another speech about our valiant purpose and how he'll singlehandedly erase the audax forever.

It'd be better if Ace nixed the speeches and actually did a mission or two on his own. As it is, the guy runs off for days and comes back with next to nothing. Finding a dried-out vial from the Black Lotus coven was his greatest achievement all year.

Breaking away from Felix, Ace saunters over in my direction. "Hey, Mako. How was your chat with Roman? Still going after the Halcyons? The Essence?"

Meaning: I'm on your team again.

"I'll find you if I want you."

"Why pretend? You're going on another mission for the Essence and I'm along for the ride. After all, I'm the best zoetic. It's only a matter of time before Roman sees it, too." Ace scans the room. "Not like there are a lot of options left for the old man."

My brows lift. "How can you look across this chamber of sick zoetic and only see competition for being Roman's favorite? That's pathetic."

"No, that's a desire to win. There's a difference." Ace marches away.

Good riddance.

Crossing the room, I kneel by Ndidi's bedside. The bloom has definitely gotten worse. A heavy cloud now surrounds my friend. Even worse, he's moaning in pain. I wave to Felix.

The medic rushes over while shoving something into the pocket of his scrubs. "Yes, Mako?"

"What's in your pocket?"

"Nothing. Is something wrong?"

I could press Felix, but Ndidi is still groaning with pain. There are priorities here. "My friend is hurting again. I thought you were giving him something for the pain."

Felix sighs. "I am."

"How about getting him some more?"

"Sure, but it won't help for long. You know how this disease is. The ones who fight the hardest end up with the most pain and shortest lifespan."

"I'm aware," I state. "Help him anyway."

Felix scurries off. A few minutes later, the medic returns with a syringe. Felix injects something into Ndidi's arm, then the medic looks to me.

"Don't worry, Mack. Ace says this is a crucible for all the zoetic. You'll find the serum and heal what's left. Only the best zoetic will survive."

I frown. "You said the ones who fight die the fastest. How can the best zoetic be folks who give up?"

"Ace says the best zoetic follow the rules and do as they're told. That's how we've always succeeded."

"Ah, I get it." Because the rules say that Ace is a senior paladin. As such, he should never answer to me.

"There." Felix pats Ndidi's shoulder. "He's out of pain for now."

And indeed, my friend's face looks far more peaceful. I take my regular place by his side and whisper words of encouragement.

"I'll help you heal, my friend."

And I will.

27

KAPS

*A*fter my audience with my parents, I have trouble falling asleep. It's not just because that low headache still bites into my temples, either.

I'm locked into Furonium for a decade, along with every other dragon shifter. If I thought folks hated me before? *Now I'm enemy number one.* No one can leave the realm and it's all my fault. I can't move two yards without someone whispering how *the PUP needs to be put down.*

To cheer myself up, I picture the intense look in Mack's blue eyes right before he kissed me.

That doesn't really help either, considering how I'll never see Mack again.

All in all, the palace never seemed so lonely.

MACK

*I*t's late by the time I launch into my briefing with Ace, Zero, Jenna and Dani.

"Our mission takes place at Devil's Park, New York," I begin. "The strike point is the L'Griffe cabin by the cliff wall. We must enter the dwelling tomorrow at midnight."

Ace doesn't ask any questions, which is highly suspicious. Makes me wonder if the guy has his own agenda. Which, let's face it, he probably does. Half the time, Ace sneaks off on missions to do *who knows what.* And as long as he isn't holding things up—like he did with the Wurtzite dagger—then I'm happy to see him go.

"No coms on this mission," I add. "This cabin is L'Griffe property. They track electronics much better than we do." I focus on Ace. "Prep up the private jet. We heading for JFK tomorrow afternoon."

"I figured that out already," adds Ace.

"The correct reply is *yes, Paladin.*"

Not be a dick, but I can't have Ace undermining me in front of the whole crew.

"Yes, Paladin," snarls Ace.

I turn to Zero. "Contact our friends in air traffic control. I don't care what it costs. We get priority take off."

"Yes, Paladin."

I shift my focus to Dani. "Wake up our FBI buddies. Get a surveillance van ready and waiting on the tarmac. We'll need a *headquarters on wheels* again."

"Yes, Paladin."

At last, I turn to Jenna. "We'll need climbing equipment to repel down the cliff wall. That must be on site in the afternoon. Usual camouflage." In my experience, putting stuff inside a fake trash bin works wonders, so long as the bin in question smells like dumpster juice.

"Everyone must wear regular body armor," I add. "And bring night goggles. We meet at the jet hangar at noon. Any questions?"

In reply, I get a smirk from Ace. The rest of the crew gives me nothing but blank stares. No doubt, I'll spend most of tomorrow morning answering the same questions over and over. It's how things go with drones.

"Good," I declare. "You know where to find me if you need me. For now, get a good night's sleep. Tomorrow will be a big day."

KAPS

S leep, you are a sneaky little bitch.
And I should know.

It's about 2 AM when I go off in search of Zin and Rhodes. I find them in the royal swimming pool, floating on their backs while figuring out the refrain to a new song. They both seem so happy in their bubble of musical creativity, I can't disturb their fun.

And yeah, maybe I feel a little sorry for myself.

The sky is starting to lighten when I decide to sneak off to my happy place. As a kid, I was a big fan of the Little Mermaid movie, especially the part where she had her own grotto tricked out with all her special human stuff that no one else understood.

I spent a lot of time in the royal treasury, which is housed in a series of caverns under the castle. You can imagine how pumped I became when I found a massive and empty stone chamber at the far end of those caves. So I tricked it out, Little Mermaid style.

That's where I am now. The place is all blue stone and holds everything I cherish in the world. I step around the space, cataloging the awesomeness that is my lair.

First of all, I keep my relic hunting outfit in a glass case because that's how Batman does it. My getup consists of hefty boots, cargo pants and a matching vest. All the pockets are filled with magical artifacts.

Sure, it's not as impressive-looking as the bat suit, but I carry much better goodies. After all, Batman just has one measly utility belt with some human stuff taped onto it. Meanwhile, my cargo pockets carry so many magical items, it isn't even funny.

Batman, eat your heart out.

I continue my inspection of the Lair Du Kaps. I have a sizable library, the shelves of which rise three stories high. As a matter of fact, I must fly up to get stuff down, which is rather badass. The less interesting books get stored up top while more important things stay on ground level. There's a system.

And the most important stuff is my collection of *El Dorado Adventures* comic books. These were made around the time the first *Superman* comics came out, only they take the man of steel, kick his ass, and rip up his cape. Opening a nearby drawer, I grab issue number seventy two and read for a bit.

After an hour of this, I'm feeling so good, I don't even notice that I'm no longer alone.

Great M has arrived.

The moment I see her, I smile from ear to ear. We share a super long hug.

"This is quite a place," says Great M.

"How did you find it?"

Great M raises her hand. A single igni lightning bolt hovers above her palm. "One guess."

I chuckle. "Your igni aren't giving you any peace, are they?"

"Nope." Great M sighs. "They say time is running out. You know where to go to find the Halcyons?"

"I know where to get started. Midnight tonight at a place called Devil's Park. Not that it does me much good." I slump onto one of the beanbags in the area I call my *pit of contemplation*. "There's no point getting worked up about it. Neither of us know magic. I'm not getting out of here."

And just like that, all my worries return with a vengeance. The dull headache that signifies the aegis web pulses with more fury. I slump deeper onto the cushy seat.

Great M plunks down onto the beanbag next to mine. "I might be able to set you free."

At that news, I sit up straighter. "But you aren't sure?"

"I told my igni I would consider helping you. That's all. It's a big step for me to ignore the wishes of your parents." Great M scans the room carefully. "My igni say this is all your stuff for fighting audax. Why haven't you told anyone what you're really up to?"

At this point, I'm dying to scream *just get me out of here already!* But Great M has her way of doing things. It's best to play along.

"I don't know."

"Bull."

This time, I outright laugh. "Fine. After Zin was taken, everyone got overprotective. Mum and Da would never let me go to Earth and hunt vampires."

Great M purses her lips. "And?"

"It's not like my people would be jumping with joy that I try to save humans, either."

Great M nods. "And?"

"Honestly, hunting audax is pretty much an obsession for me. I'm not sure why I'm so driven about it." I carefully keep the Lone Vigilante thing to myself. There are some things even Great M doesn't need to know.

"Fair enough." She smacks her lips. "Who's the guy?"

"Guy?" My voice comes out all nervous and screechy. "There's no guy."

"That's not what the igni say."

"They're really nosy."

"No kidding."

"His name is Mack."

"And is he your rhana?"

I shake my head. "He's human."

"So he's not your rhana, but you fight vampires for him as a dragon."

I sit upright, my mouth open with shock. "That was one time."

Great M tilts her head. I've seen this movement before; she's listening to her igni. "Someone disagrees. One guess who."

"Tell your igni to butt out. It was only once. Really." I scooch closer to Great M. "What are they saying about Mack?"

Is it a little contradictory to tell the igni to buzz off and then ask for details? Sure, but this could be my only chance for Mack-related intel, ever. Just because I'm never seeing him again doesn't mean I'm not curious.

"Before, they said you *went dragon* to keep this guy alive. Now, my igni just keep repeating, *she fights for Mack*, over and over."

I slump back onto my beanbag. "That's really not helpful."

Great M rubs her palms together before rising. That perks me up. A *palm rub and stand* combination means she's made her decision.

I move to stand beside her. "What do you think?" I don't need to add the part about *getting me out of here.*

"As your Great M, I see it as my sacred duty to empower you to kick ass and find covens."

"Like the Halcyons?"

"Maybe. If there weren't an aegis web on Furonium, could you get to Earth?"

"Hells, yeah."

"I mean from this very lair of yours. You can't fly off a rooftop and wing through one of the sky portals. Do you have a magic ring to make say, a ghoul portal?"

"I've got better. Ghoul rings carry only one charge." I bob my brows. "I carry a magic mirror in my cargo vest. It transports me anywhere, so long as I give it time to recharge between trips."

"Cool." Great M shoots me a thumbs up. Her tail does the same, using the arrowhead end as a modified hand. Not sure how Great M got so lucky with her tail, but she did.

"So how will you get me past the aegis web?" I ask. "You can't break Mum's spell."

"No, but I have some very anxious igni on my side. You know I create soul columns to move spirits to Heaven and Hell, right?"

"Sure."

"If I make one here and keep it steady, then you can stand inside. That will put you in a null space. Not Heaven. Not Hell. Not anything. You won't be subject to the spell."

I bob a little on the balls of my feet. "Wow. This is great!"

"One more thing. My igni state that for this to work, you must work in secret. No one from the after-realms can help you, not even me." She steps closer. "You don't have to listen to my igni, though. This is your choice, Kaps. Does that make sense?"

I picture Mack. And the zoetic. And Mack some more. They could all die without this serum.

"If I stay here, I'll never forgive myself."

Great M shoots me a sly smile. "So it is a choice."

I'd always seen fighting audax as a something I felt forced to do. Yet Great M is spot on. I could stay in Furonium if I wanted to. I'd just be miserable as Hell.

With this realization, something inside me unfurls. "I guess you're right, Great M."

"I'm always right; that's the best part about being

me." She gives me one of her most dazzling and goddess-like smiles. "Want to know a secret?"

I nod.

"I think you can do this. Find the Halcyon coven. Kick some audax butt. Work stuff out with your human. The whole magilla, Kaps."

"I'm not so sure."

Great M takes my hands in hers. "I was like you once. I had a secret life, only mine was full of demons and arena battles. No one wanted to hear about it, least of all your Great Grandmother. Other kids called me names. Even my best friend thought I was out of my mind."

"Cissy? Really?"

"Oh, yeah. Cis said I had a compulsion. But I thought of it more as a calling. Turns out, I was right." She winks. "Again."

I shiver. Now that it's coming down to actually traveling to Earth, my stomach is doing flip flops. "I'm scared, Great M."

"That's part of the deal. But know this. The worst part is behind you. You've hidden your heart's true passion and kept it alive. Now's the time to make a decision. Do you turn away or walk the path? Is this a compulsion or a calling?"

"I suppose it's whatever I want it to be."

"Right answer," declares Great M.

I quickly change into my cargo pants and vest, taking care to pack both with all my best magical junk. Great M summons a column of igni and damn, it's a beautiful sight. The many tiny lightning bolts swirl around in a pillar of brightness and energy.

After stepping inside the column, I pull out my magic mirror from a pocket of my cargo vest. It's a compact model that's about the size of a silver dollar. After flipping the cover open, I find that the mirror inside glows with blue light, meaning it's charged and ready to use.

Gripping the round item in my palms, I picture the name of my destination: *Devil's Park, New York.* With that image in mind, I speak the magic words.

> *Magic mirror in my hand*
> *Take me to the needed land.*

Blue mist pours out from the small mirror. Within seconds, I'm completely surrounded in an enchanted haze. My entire body vibrates as the transportation spell kicks in.

The last thing I hear is Great M's voice calling to me.

"Kick ass, Baby!"

And I smile.

MACK

*I*t's a long day of rounding up gear and answering questions from the crew, but at last I'm in position at Devil's Park. I check my watch.

11:47 PM

Pausing by the cliff's upper ledge, I gaze down into the valley below. A dark forest stretches off into the distance. Overhead, a full moon hangs in a sky filled with stars. Behind me stretches a large—and mostly empty—parking lot that's bordered by dense forest.

Kneeling down, I check my gear. Five ropes still dangle down the cliff wall and into the valley below. Flipping down my night goggles, I scan down into the darkness. The cabin is there, right below me, just as Gage promised. Looks deserted, too, which is even better. From here, my mission is simple.

Descend to the cabin.

Seal off the perimeter.

Get the relic.

But I have yet to start things. My strike team still isn't here. Again.

At last, our van pulls up. Jessa and Dani step out, both of them dressed in black.

"Where are Ace and Zero?" I ask.

"I don't know," says Jessa. "They left before we did."

I clench my hands into fists. If I don't punch at least Ace tonight, it'll be a miracle.

KAPS

Traveling by magic mirror is the bomb.
My favorite relic drops me off right by a sign that reads *Devil's Park*. Hefty trees stretch off in every direction, all the stout trunks and twisty branches concealed in shadows. A handful of moonbeams cut through the leaves, sending pale lines of light angling toward the forest floor.

The sign comes complete with a handy map. There's only one cabin by a cliff wall and it's a short walk from this very spot. I check my watch.

11:55 PM

Five minutes left to reach the cabin. I stride off in the fastest direction.

Relic, come to Kaps.

Because that's what this is about.

Relics.

Witches.

A noble love of humanity.

It has nothing to do with the prospect of seeing Mack again.

And if my stomach is doing somersaults? *Total coincidence.*

I pick up the pace to a run.

Suddenly, my boot snags on something. Pin wheeling my arms, I hop about. It isn't easy, but I somehow regain my balance. Looking around, I eyeball what almost made me face-plant.

A dead body.

Oh, no.

32

MACK

1 1:57 PM

At last, Zero runs up from the line of trees. "Where have you guys been?" asks Zero. "I've been hailing you on the com forever."

"No coms on this mission," I command. "We covered that already. What's the problem?"

"Ace ran off," declares Zero.

"Which is something he does all the time," I counter.

"He said something about an audax in the woods. We have to go after him."

I hold up my hand. "No. The mission parameters are clear. We must reach that cabin at midnight. And if there are audax around, I can assure you that Ace is hauling ass in the opposite direction."

"Come on," says Zero. "There are zoetic rules that go

beyond missions. We can't risk someone as important as Ace, *Mako*."

"We're burning time here." I point down to the valley below. "Gage told us to be in that cabin at midnight. I agree that we must protect our fellow zoetic. And the best way to do that is by securing Gage's relic."

"Well, I'm going after Ace," says Zero.

I round on Jessa and Dani. "Take Zero to the van and get out of here."

Zero tries to fight, but Jessa knocks him out in five seconds flat. In short order, Zero gets dragged off. Less than a minute later, the van peels off into the night.

With the drama over, I pull on my face mask, grab my rope and get ready to repel down. *So typical for Ace to run off right before a mission. What a waste of space that guy is.*

Suddenly, a new figure limps out of the shadows.

It's a park ranger. "I'm hurt." He reaches for me. "Can you help me?"

I sigh. "I can see through your glamour, you know. It doesn't matter that it's dark out."

"Ah, well," says the audax. "It was worth a try."

Looking past the glamour, I spy a decaying corpse under the park ranger illusion. Only one audax wears a torn WWII uniform with a black eye patch.

"Hello, Carnage."

"All alone, Mack?"

"Not really." I picture the golden stake that's holstered at my shin. If I can get this quickly into the vampire's chest, then I'll be set.

Carnage opens his mouth and hisses, a motion that causes his fangs to get highlighted in the moonlight. Raising his arm, Carnage shows off the long dagger gripped in his right fist.

And he races right for me.

33

KAPS

his park ranger guy can't be dead.
        Maybe he's still breathing.
Like very, very shallow breaths.

I kneel beside the body that literally tripped me up. It's a young guy with tanned skin and curly blond hair. He wears a green jacket-n-pants combo that seems standard for all park rangers.

And there are puncture holes on his neck.

Sadly, this isn't the first time I've found a body like this one. Skin lies loose on his frame—it's the result of his blood being drained. An audax vampire just drank this poor man's blood.

I picture what will happen next. Humans will find this body. To them, it will appear as if this guy had a heart attack and that will be the end of it.

In truth, it's another life taken by a vampire. Which means it's all the more important to help the zoetic.

I simply must reach that cabin, find the relic and get those Halcyon witches brewing up help.

34

MACK

*C*arnage slams into me, knocking me over the side of the cliff. As I topple backwards, I grip onto my repelling rope with my left hand. There's a moment of weightlessness followed by the slam of pain in my left arm and shoulder as gravity kicks in. The rope cuts into my palm but I'm able to stay tethered in place.

Which is a good thing. It's a five-story drop to the ground.

Looking up, I see Carnage looming by the top ledge of the cliff. He's still wearing the glamour spell that makes him look like a park ranger, so I have the illusion I can see both of them at once.

That poor human.

Carnage raises his right arm, showing off how he holds one of the other ropes I set up for my crew.

And he leaps down toward me.

Carnage swoops down at an angle, hoping to use both gravity and a pendulum-style force to propel his boots right into my kidneys. I wait until he inches away and then drop down a few yards on my rope. The movement does a number on my hands, but Carnage ends up kicking the cliff wall instead of my stomach.

Reaching down, I pull out my handy golden stake from the holster on my calf. Gripping the weapon in my free hand, I get ready for the next round of attacks.

Sure enough, Carnage swings over to grab my own rope line. Keeping one rope in each hand, he slides down, his boots aiming right for my skull.

Good plan, that.

At the last moment, I leap off my rope and cling onto the cliff wall. The motion keeps Carnage from kicking in my head. Sadly, I must let go of my golden stake in the process. The glittering metal weapon flies off to the woods. Chances are, I'll never see it again.

Things aren't going well. Carnage now has two lines. I'm nowhere near any of the other repelling ropes and my only weapon is toast.

And there's still a four-story drop below me.

35

KAPS

J step through a line of trees and into a small clearing. A few yards ahead, a lopsided structure stands before a towering cliff wall.

Found it. The L'Griffe cabin.

And it's midnight on the nose. *Go me.*

The dwelling is a jumble of cockeyed wooden boards, janky nails and tar. Moonlight glints off the dirty windows. Stepping inside, I find a large and empty room that holds a massive fireplace. Dozens of boxes stand stacked against one wall. A few dusty chairs line the floor. The place looks totally deserted.

Distant thuds and grunts sound from far above me. Audax must still on the hunt. Guess killing that park ranger wasn't enough for them. There's no time to waste and a single question to ask.

Where's that relic anyway?

I've been in situations like this one before. Sometimes people get fancy and hide things under floorboards or behind a loose fireplace brick. That's rare. More often that not, folks just jam stuff in a box without knowing it has any value. So that's where I start my search.

I yank open the nearest container. For some reason, it's stuffed with cleaning supplies. Not sure why they need eight cans of Comet in a deserted cabin, but it seems they do. There's also soap and a bunch of scrub brushes. Someone in L'Griffe must be a neatnik.

The next box is packed with *do it yourself* junk. There are rolls of duct tape. Cans of spray glue. And way too much string. What's this all about? Are the L'Griffe doing arts and crafts in the woods? I'm about to move on to the next container when I see it.

A small manilla envelope sits at the bottom of the box.

Come to Kaps.

At last, here's something interesting. I scoop up the envelope and my tail slices it open. Reaching inside, I pull out something that's both unexpected and awesome.

No, it's not a recipe for Essence.

But it is a comic book.

And not just any comic book, but the very first issue of *El Dorado Adventures*. As in the only thing missing from my collection. I grip the publication against my chest.

Issue number one, how I've dreamt of you!

With trembling fingers, I gingerly open the cover. Sure enough, there's the Sentinel, a warrior who has taken upon himself to protect the magical city of El Dorado. The Sentinel wears brown body leathers and a perma-scowl on his tanned face. He trudges along a deserted beach. A thought bubble hovers above his head.

I have been summoned to protect El Dorado, thinks the Sentinel.

Suddenly, the words on the page change.

I squint.

Do a double take.

And pull the comic in for a closer look.

Sure enough, the text has completely transformed. The thought bubble no longer reads, *I have been summoned to protect El Dorado.*

Now the Sentinel thinks, *I can lead you to the Halcyon's den.*

My eyes widen with shock. The creators of the *El Dorado Adventures* didn't just catch some of the vibe from the Halcyon. They clearly caught some of the magic as well.

This is so cool, I can't stand it.

The thought bubble changes once again. *You must take me and go.*

"Go?" I ask.

My mind captures a snapshot of this moment. Am I really hanging out in an empty cabin while talking to a comic book?

Why yes, yes I am.

The word bubble beside the Sentinel answers my question.

Leave, it reads. *NOW.*

No need to tell me twice. I speed toward door.

BOOM!

The ceiling implodes. Two guys tumble through and onto the cabin floor. Their bodies are locked in hand-to-hand combat.

At this point, I really should leave. After all, the igni sent me here for a relic, which I now have in my possession. My personal hero, the Sentinel, just told me to leave via a magic comic that's probably powered by none other than the Halcyon coven.

And I would exit, except I catch the faces of the two men who just fell through the ceiling.

One is the same guy I just tripped over in the forest. And since I can see through glamours, I can detect an audax underneath the fake skin. Carnage. He's a rather bad boy.

And the second guy is none other than Mack.

Intense emotions sweep through me. One second, my body feel light as a feather. *Mack is here!* The next moment, my blood boils with rage.

No one touches my human.

Suddenly, I know the perfect way to take Carnage down. I rush over to the second box and get to work.

Time to summon my inner sneaky bitch.

36

MACK

*A*ll my senses have collapsed into a single point of focus.

Carnage.

Back when he was human, Carnage was a Nazi shock trooper. That means he was trained to use every tool in the military arsenal in order to break through enemy lines. Decades of drinking human blood have made those skills even more powerful.

I can't take my eyes off the guy *or else*. At some point, our battle slid down the cliff wall and landed inside the L'Griffe cabin. Some small voice in the back of my head says that my mission is to find a relic inside this place.

More of me wants to stay alive, though. And without a golden stake, that's looking tricker by the second.

I scan the room, looking for something else I can use in this battle.

Then I see her.

Kaps.

This is an awful situation. I'm beat to Hell and fighting one of the most powerful audax ever. And yet there's no missing the jolt of pure joy that now reverberates through my nervous system.

Kaps is here.

Even better, she's fishing around in the nearby boxes. No doubt, she's scheming to help take down Carnage.

Perfect.

Carnage swings his dagger toward me. I leap backward; his swipe hits nothing but air.

I glance over to Kaps. She's spraying glue onto some small object in her palm.

"Fireplace, Mack!" she calls.

"Got it!"

Leaning over, I ram my shoulder into Carnage's stomach, knocking him right into the fireplace.

"Back up!" cries Kaps.

I leap away from the fireplace as something speeds over my head. From the corner of my eye, I make out what Kaps was working on. She's glued a zippo lighter to the side of a pressurized can of highly flammable glue.

My brows lift. *That'll do it.*

The makeshift bomb lands next to Carnage with a soft clunk. The vampire stares at the item for a moment, his face crumpled with confusion. I use the break to rush over to Kaps, curling her smaller body under my larger one.

Ka-BOOM!

The bomb explodes, slamming Carnage against the back wall of the fireplace. Every inch of him is encased in flame. He howls with pain and anger.

Kaps pulls her golden stake from a holster in her calf. She rises from under my protection of my body to stride over to Carnage. Leaning over, she stabs the old vampire right through the heart.

Even though Carnage is encased in fire, there's no missing the golden glow of magic that now surrounds him as well.

"The Elector will make you pay," howls Carnage.

"The Elector can kiss my ass," counters Kaps.

An even brighter flare of golden light now surrounds Carnage. When the brightness vanishes, the fireplace is filled with ash.

"Serves you right," grumbles Kaps. "Going after Mack."

At this point, I'm not sure what's hotter. The makeshift bomb? How Kaps stabbed the vampire? Or the line about Carnage deserving death for attacking me?

Hard to say.

Kaps turns around. She's all things fierce and lovely in her treasure hunter's uniform. Her dark hair hangs in wild tendrils around her face.

Our gazes lock. My heart functions again. *Joy. Relief. Desire.* So many things reel through my body, it's hard to keep track. I step closer. "You keep saving my life."

A pretty blush colors her cheeks. "I do, don't I?" Her face lights up with all kinds of happy. I want nothing more than to find more ways to make that grin reappear.

I huff out a long breath. "I don't have lots of time, sadly. I still need to finish my mission." I scan the room. "There's a relic in here in that I'm supposed to find."

"Well, I've another surprise for you. Lookie here." From her vest pocket, Kaps pulls out a comic. The name of the series is *El Dorado Adventures.*

I take a half step backward. "Where did you get that?"

She nods toward the wall. "One of those boxes."

I shake my head. "That can't be right. Every copy of *El Dorado Adventures* got destroyed ages ago."

"That's not exactly true." Kaps winks. "Wait until you see what this thing can do." She pulls out the comic book and shows me a page. Text changes before my eyes.

Place me there with the rest
Then I shall show you all the best

I frown. "What does that mean?"

"This is an easy one, Sherlock. I've collected all the other comic books in this series, except for this one. If we place this issue with the others then—*bippity boppity boo*—it will show us how to reach the Halcyons."

"Let me guess. Your collection is in Furonium."

Kaps slips the comic book into her pocket. "That's the place."

"In that case, I'm going with you."

Kaps shakes her head. "We talked about this. I'm not ready to work with anyone else."

"And it's not safe for you to work alone. I may be a weak human, but no one's finished more successful zoetic missions than I have. Even Gage turns to me when he has a tricky problem."

Kaps half rolls her eyes. "Like me?"

"Of course, like you. You're amazing beyond words. I was damned lucky to capture you in the first place. And watching you fight those audax?" I ball my hands into fists. "It was the most beautiful and terrifying thing I'd ever seen."

Kaps sighs. "I don't know, Mack."

"I do. Seeing you fly away was one of the worst moments of my life. Knowing you were facing trouble alone? Awful. I want to respect your decisions, Kaps. And I tried that route when I let you go before. But I don't have it in me to do that twice. Wherever you go, I'll have your back. You might as well plan on it, because it's happening."

Kaps keeps staring at the floor. I step closer. "What are you thinking?" Reaching forward, I rest my fingertips against her jawline. Little by little, I guide her gaze toward mine. Her eyes glisten with tears.

"Talk to me, Kaps. Please."

"Why would you feel this way about me?"

"How can anyone *not* be in awe of you? From the first moment I watched you on the dance floor, you awakened life in me. Even now I can't believe someone as strong and lovely as you roams the world. That's something I must protect."

Kaps reaches up and grasps my wrist. "Okay. If you're following me anyway, I guess I'll allow you to adventure near me. But we aren't a team or anything."

"Good." I exhale. "So how are we getting to Furonium?"

"There was a aegis web spell, but my parents took it down."

"How do you know?"

Kaps taps her temples. "My magical headache disappeared. My family must have removed aegis web when I escaped. That way, they can send search parties to Earth." She pulls a small round mirror from a pocket of her vest. "The bad news is, there isn't enough of a charge on my magic mirror to send both of us back to my palace. But the good news is, we can just fly there."

"We?"

"Ever ridden a girl like me?" Kaps' eyes bulge. "That came out wrong. Have you ever gone bareback?" Kaps sets her hands over her face. "Oh, crap."

It takes an effort not to laugh out loud. "I have never traveled via dragon, if that's what you mean."

"It is. Thank you."

And in this moment, all is perfect in the world. I started off this morning with an empty soul and hopeless task ahead of me.

But with Kaps on my side, anything is possible.

37

KAPS

*M*ack and I step outside so I can transform. The cabin is trashed enough as it is. Using my magic mirror, I send my cherished cargo clothes back to my secret lair. There's enough of a charge for that, at least. I can pick them up later on.

After all, this isn't my first time sneaking back home.

With that done, I change into my dragon self. I'm about to explain the best way to get onto a dragon's back when Mack climbs up like a pro.

Do I sense his thighs against me? I do.

And yes, it's super distracting.

Still, I take to the skies and find the nearest portal-cloud to Furonium. Although the aegis web is down, that doesn't mean I can saunter through the front door of my family's palace.

It's sneaky little bitch time again.

The Northwest wing of the palace has been under construction for months. My old bedchamber with my sisters is there. The room is totally deserted and therefore ideal for stealing in and out. Plus, part of the rebuild included adding the perfect-sized balcony for dragon landings.

That's my next stop.

It's not too long of a trip from Earth to Furonium. By the time Mack and I arrive, it's close to dawn. That's the perfect hour to sneak into the palace, mostly because the Kathikon guards change shifts at sunrise. Often the guards are more concerned bout how the last group needs to clean up after themselves than what's soaring overhead.

After winging my way over the forest behind the palace, I land on my super secret balcony. Mack slides off my back. My inner dragon grumbles at his loss.

Turning to Mack, I hold my clawed finger over my maw in the universal symbol for quiet. He nods. I then loop my finger in a circle. The meaning is unspoken but clear, *turn around.*

Now do dragon shifters usually care about nudity? That's a big *no.* But Mack isn't just anyone.

I change back to my human form and dig around in a nearby clothes bin. I always hide bathrobes on this balcony for just such occasions. If anyone asks why I'm in the Northwest wing, I can then lie and say I was using the pools here.

Like I said, I have a system.

At first, I don't see any bathrobes. It takes a little searching, but I finally scrounge one up from the bottom of the bin.

Some small voice warns me that this means something, but I ignore it. I've enough to worry about without nitpicking the palace staff for cleaning out linens from the balconies.

Once I'm set, I focus once again on Mack. "Ready."

He turns to face me, then looks me over from head to toe. The way he stares at me, you'd think I was wearing a fancy ballgown instead of a bathrobe.

A girl could get used to looks like that.

Stop it, Kaps. You aren't even friends.

I step inside my old bedroom. Growing up, this chamber seemed so vast. Now, it's a snug place with lots of pink and purple everywhere. Outside of the new balcony, the room has been kept as a shrine to our childhood.

Not that I'm complaining.

Something draws me to check out the far dark corner of the room—the very place where my big girl bed was kept. An image appears in my mind. It's Goldilocks.

As I step closer, I realize why that particular picture appeared.

Someone is sleeping in my bed.

I stop in my tracks. "Zin?"

My twin leaps up from the mattress. "Kaps!" She's lovely as ever with her white locks and bright eyes. We share a long hug. Even after everything she's been through, Zin is still as open and bright-eyed as ever.

And yes, she's wearing one of my balcony bath robes. Figures.

Rhodes sits up beside her. "Hey." He stretches. Like Zin, he's in a bathrobe. Unlike Zin, Rhodes has short brown hair and a powerful build.

"Hey, Rhodes." I sense more than see Mack move so he now stands behind me.

Rhodes shakes his head. "Told you, Zin."

Zin breaks our hug. "My Rhodes said that if you came back, you would land here first."

I shrug. "Rhodes would know." For years, Rhodes was my body guard. He still knows my systems.

Rhodes hops out of bed. "You're back at last." He rolls his eyes. "You can't keep pulling this stuff, especially with Huntress on retreat."

Mack steps forward. "What did you say?"

Rhodes shrugs. "Come on, random guy. Kaps is Kaps."

Mack stalks closer. "You have no idea who Kaps is and what she does."

Rhodes' tail arcs behind him. *Battle stance.* "I'm a dragon shifter. You're human. Keep talking and this won't end well for you."

Fast as a whip, *Mack the human* kicks *Rhodes the dragon shifter* smack behind his kneecaps. My old bodyguard tumbles onto his ass.

I gasp. After all, I'd seen Mack move quickly back in the cabin, but there was other stuff going on. Watching him now? There's definitely something not-too-human about him.

Whatever smidgeon of demon DNA Mack inherited, it's a doozie.

38

MACK

I loom over the smart-mouthed dragon guy. "You were saying?"

Kaps' twin steps between us. "Please, my Rhodes. Kaps has just returned. Do not ruin this."

Rhodes slowly rises while keeping his gaze locked on me. This guy doesn't trust what I'll do next.

He's right not to.

"What are you?" asks Rhodes.

"Zoetic."

"Never heard of that."

"I'm not surprised." *Considering how no one here figured out what Kaps really does with her time.*

Kaps links her arm with mine. "The zoetic are a secret society of human warriors. Many have a little demonic DNA in their past, isn't that right, Mack?"

I nod. "Something like that."

"What's your game?" asks Rhodes. "I know the kinds of humans that Kaps attracts."

Rage tightens up my neck and shoulders. This guy keeps talking about Kaps like she hasn't single handedly saved countless human lives.

"You were Kaps' guard?" I ask.

"Twenty-four hours a day, seven days a week. For years."

"And you sound proud of that fact."

Rhodes lifts his chin. "You bet I am."

"Yet you don't know the first thing about her."

"Hey, I kept her out of a castle tower. That way, she could play rock star and hunt magical trinkets on Earth."

When I speak, my voice carries the edge of a roar. "Wrong!"

Rhodes turns to Kaps. "What is this human talking about?"

My gaze locks with Kaps. She's worrying her lower lip with her teeth. I haven't known her for long, but I can tell one thing, Kaps is debating about telling her family the truth.

Maybe it will be a good thing. Or Kaps can keep hiding. Yet whatever she decides, Kaps has my support.

Protecting the princess? That I can do. Telling the truth is her call.

So I wait.

39

KAPS

This is the moment. I could share everything. Or keep my true self hidden away some more.

Do I set the Lone Vigilante loose?

Mack's entire body vibrates with pent-up rage. He wants to scream at Rhodes, but he's holding back for me. Somehow, that gives me the strength I need.

"Here's the situation," I begin. "There are vampires called audax who hunt humans. I look for supernatural relics, sure. But that's because I need them to find and fight those vampires."

"Let me get this straight," says Rhodes. "You've been protecting humans all this time."

Zin's face pales. "From vampires."

I force my shoulders to straighten. "That's right."

"It's what the zoetic do as well," adds Mack.

"You must keep all this a secret," I add. "The zoetic have been hit with a magical illness. Mack and I are looking for a potion to heal them. That's why we're here."

Rhodes shakes his head. "But your parents are frantic. There are rumors someone's out to kidnap you. Can't we tell them anything?"

"No," I state firmly. "I already tried to explain things to them. Or rather, Great M tried. She told Mum and Da that her igni want me to find a coven on Earth that brews this healing serum. They didn't listen."

Zin steps to stand by Rhodes' side. "I don't know, Kaps."

"But Great M believes in me." I hate that my voice has a little wobble to it.

Mack grips my waist with more force. "And I believe in her, too."

Warmth and affection spread through my chest. I've been so obsessed with protecting myself from getting hurt, it never occurred to me how good it would feel to have a true ally by my side.

Zin forces a smile. "Then I shall try to have faith in you as well."

Rhodes doesn't answer. Instead, my old bodyguard

eyes Mack with distaste. "Anyone think this guy will protect Kaps?"

"Look," declares Mack. "I get it. You don't see me as equal to a shifter. But it doesn't change the facts here. Kaps will do what she thinks is right. Try to stop her, and you'll need to take me down first."

Did I say it feels good to have an ally? It's pretty freaking great.

"Here's the deal," I state. "Mack and I must get something from the royal vaults. Then we'll return to Earth. Will you try to stop us?"

Zin and Rhodes slowly shake their heads. That was easier than I expected, so I decide to go for the close.

"And will you keep our secrets?"

Zin and Rhodes share a look. Tension bites into my temples. If Rhodes and Zin blab to my parents, then this mission is over. Long seconds tick by with no answer.

At last, Zin is the one to break the silence. "We'll give you forty-eight hours."

"But after that," says Rhodes, "we'll burn Earth down if we have to."

Now Mack and I share a long look. His blue eyes seem to glimmer with hope.

We're really doing this.

I refocus on Zin and Rhodes. "Agreed."

Best to get to get out of here before anyone changes

their minds. Turning to nearby wall, I press a panel. A door opens.

Zin gasps. "How long has a hidden door been there?"

"Since we were kids. Even Huntress never found it." Zin and Rhodes look completely stunned. And I must admit, it's a slightly satisfying sight.

"It's like I told you," says Mack. "You don't know the first thing about the *real Kaps*."

"I'm starting to get that idea," whispers Rhodes.

"Be safe!" calls Zin.

Nodding, I step into the darkness of the passageway.

MACK

*K*aps and I march through a maze of deserted stone tunnels. With each step forward, our path angles deeper underground.

Clearly, Kaps knows these passages well. She dodges pools of muck and random mini-boulders with ease. Once again, I'm reminded of how Kaps appeared when I first saw her on the dance floor. Everything about this woman simply exudes confidence and energy.

Kaps and I speed through a final set of twists and turns. At last, the dark and cramped tunnels open to a tall chamber made from blue granite.

It's stunning.

Entering this space is like walking inside an obelisk. Four slim walls tower around me, ending in a small pyramid shape up top. Two of those walls are covered with shelves of books. The others are lined with blue metal drawers of all shapes and sizes, a pattern which fits together in an intricate mosaic.

At the center of the floor sits a circle of beanbag chairs. There's also a tall glass case with Kaps' cargo vest and pants displayed inside, superheroine style.

Stretching her arms, Kaps steps around in a slow circle. "Welcome to my lair," she announces.

"This is amazing, Kaps."

She blinks with mock-humility. "Do you *really* think so?"

"I collect stuff myself, but nothing like this."

"Well, I am a dragon. Hoarding is our job." She gestures to the walls of drawers. "All my artifacts are in here." She then points in the opposite direction. "And those are my books."

"And the *El Dorado Adventures*? Are those books or artifacts?"

"Excellent question." Her eyes positively glimmer with excitement. "I debated the same issue myself. In the end, I decided that they count as artifacts." She saunters over to a large square drawer that sits near floor level. "My collection sits in here."

Kaps tightens the tie on her robes. Not for the first time, I try not to think about how she's naked under that garment.

Nope, not thinking about it at all.

Much.

My *not-thinking* about Kaps is somewhat consuming, because the next thing I know, Kaps has gone over to her superheroine-style glass case, opened up one side and pulled out the new comic book from her vest.

Handy thing, that magic mirror. Sends people and things with amazing accuracy.

"Here we go!" announces Kaps. She steps back over to the opposite wall and pulls on the handle for a large square drawer. Stacks of comic books sit inside. Kaps places her latest acquisition on top.

Suddenly, all the books fly out from the drawer, spinning in the air like tops. *Magic.* Each one splits into individual pages which then reform into a hollow and unmistakable shape.

A wyvern.

41

KAPS

There's a comic-book wyvern in my lair.

Wow. Just wow.

Wyverns are similar dragons in that they can fly. Where wyverns differ is that their wings are attached under their arms.

Pretty badass, really.

And this particular wyvern is a magical creation made out of comic books.

So there's that.

A memory appears. As a kid, I once made paper-mâché model of a dragon. Only mine was a three-foot long number made from leftover wrapping paper and glue.

This is totally different. It's large as a house, hollow inside, and crinkles as it moves.

And did I mention this Wyvern is also rocking a sphinx vibe? It is. The thing has a human head instead of a dragon-style one. Bonus.

"You wish to see us?" asks the wyvern.

"That depends," I reply. "Are you one of the Halcyons?"

"I am. My form was not always this way."

In other words, she was human once. *There's a story here, that's for sure.*

The wyvern lifts her chin. Her human face is a round with puckered lips and big eyes. She also sports the kind of way-piled-up-on-your-head style of hair that women liked in the late 1800's.

"My appearance displeases you," says the wyvern.

"No, you look great." I turn to Mack. "Doesn't she look fabulous?"

"Sure." Mack nods. "Absolutely."

Wow. That wasn't too convincing.

"I am called Ratna," announces the wyvern. "You may visit me, Aveza and Khushi tomorrow at sunrise. We are the Halcyon coven." She lifts her arms, showing off the papery wings that connect to her torso.

She really is a massive dragon. Er, wyvern.

Ratna flaps her arms, creating a fast-moving wind inside my lair. Not gonna lie. There's a moment where I panic that my stuff might get ruined. But the books and drawers stay put. Although my Batman-style outfit case does wobble a bit. Other than that, no problem.

When Ratna is done flapping, there's a new item sitting on the floor of my lair.

A small golden ingot.

I go to pick it up because TREASURE.

"No!" snaps Ratna. "That is for Mack."

Now, anyone else might back off at this point. I mean, the big bad wyvern-sphinx is getting ticked off again. But I've spent years hoarding every little bit of magical junk I can lay my hands on.

Plus, this is my lair.

And I am a dragon.

I step closer. *That ingot is mine.*

"Take that and I shall curse you," bellows Ratna.

Then again, maybe backing off doesn't suck.

"Got it." I stop in my tracks. "How about *you* grab the ingot, Mack?"

"My pleasure." As Mack saunters past me, he shoots me a glance filled with sarcastic glee.

Fine. Yeah. He's getting the treasure. Whatever.

Mack scoops up the small ingot. To my eye, the thing resembles a half-melted marble. So what if it's gold? It's not the best treasure in the world.

Okay. I totally want that ingot.

Once Ratna sees that Mack holds the ingot, she grins, exposing a mouth filled with pointy teeth.

"Place that ingot into the ocean tomorrow at sunrise," says Ratna.

I raise my hand. "Question."

Ratna glares in my direction. "Mack must be the one to place the ingot in the water."

"Oh." *She guessed it, all right.*

Mack gives me another entry from his sarcastic side-eye collection. "Was that your question?"

"No. Maybe. Yes, it was totally my question."

"Until dawn," says Ratna.

Ratna's comic book body burst into a flurry of colorful pages. The sheets flutter about for bit before reforming into the full books. The titles reset themselves neatly into the proper drawer.

Nice.

After the massive paper monster that was Ratna, my lair seems positively silent and empty.

Mack sets the ingot into his pocket. "Seems we have until tomorrow morning."

I scrunch up my face. "Let's not hang around. Mum could cast a spell, figure out I'm here, and the we're both stuck in Furonium."

"So we fly back?" asks Mack.

"That would be best."

"I'd like to visit the Fortress once we return, if that's all right with you."

"Of course." *He wants to see the other zoetic.*

"It's probably best if I enter the healing chambers alone."

I tap my cheek. "What did you say to me once?" I lift my pointer finger. "Ah, I have it. *I'm going with you.* But we're not partners. I'm there more as an uninvolved observer."

Mack gives me another sly smile. "Thank you, Kaps."

I want to leap forward and wrap Mack in a hug. But I'm able to stop myself in time. I'm just on the same mission with Mack. We're not *together*-together. And I'm definitely not developing more feelings for him.

Visiting the Fortress is nothing more than a kind gesture I'm doing for a mostly-random guy who is in need.

Who kidnapped me.

But then I protected him as a dragon.

And now it's all very, very casual.

42

MACK

Kaps leads us through another set of hidden passageways. Within minutes, we pass through a hidden door and step out into a heavy forest. From there, Kaps sets her clothes into what's called a magic bag of holding. It's basically a small pouch that expands to fit whatever you need.

On a side note, it's getting tougher not to look at Kaps during these episodes of nakedness.

In no time, I've got the bag of holding slung over my shoulder and dragon Kaps flying beneath me. As we soar away, I explain how to reach the Fortress. Unlike humans, Kaps will see the large stone structure from the sky.

It's a long flight, but eventually we land on the beach

behind the Fortress. There's more not-looking as a naked Kaps changes back into her cargo stuff.

I may be up for sainthood after this mission.

For months, marching into the Fortress has been about as much fun as a burst appendix. Yet with Kaps at my side, the walk isn't so terrible. I actually want to show where I've spent my life.

As we march up the front steps, I rest my hand on the small of her back. It's not like she can't find the front door without any help, but it seems like the gentlemanly thing to do.

And yes, I'm making up excuses to touch her.

Kaps shoots me a shy smile as we reach the door proper. She likes contact as well, only she needs to take things slowly. I'm fine with that. And if it doesn't end in us being more than friends? I can handle that as well. Kaps is my sunshine; I need her in my life any way I can get her.

No one waits in the reception chamber. Which makes sense. At this hour, everyone should be at afternoon training. Except for Ace, that is. He'll be in Roman's lab, brainstorming new ways to suck up to our Liege.

I guide Kaps down the hallway that leads to the healing chamber. Once there, my heart sinks. A familiar sight greets me: hundreds of zoetic, all of them unconscious. Crimson-colored haze surrounds each body. The groans of pain have never been louder.

Felix leans over a nearby cot. As soon as we enter, he looks up from what he was doing. The expression on his face can be described in a single word: *guilty*.

"Mack," says Felix. "We weren't expecting you. And you brought a friend."

"What were you doing just then?" I ask.

"Oh, regular stuff, that's all."

For a moment, the red mist rises as it takes another form. Something seems to hover above each bed. I've never witnessed anything like this before, but there's no mistaking what these shapes resemble.

Ghosts.

"What is that?" I nod toward the beds. Yet as soon as the ghostly forms appear, they vanish.

Felix quickly scans from left to right. It's another entry from the Big Book of Guilty Looks. "I'm human. I didn't see anything."

Kaps raises her hand. "I saw it."

"Ghosts, right?" I ask.

"Something like that. Great M moves human souls. They aren't red, though. I'm not sure what those were. That said, I spend most of my time in Furonium, so I've only seen Great M do her thing a few times. For all I know, ghosts are color coded."

"Let's keep this between us," Felix lowers his voice to the barest whisper. "The bloom creates odd illusions around certain people. Ace says to hide things like this from Roman. We don't want our Liege getting upset."

"What is happening, exactly?" I ask.

"Nothing," replies Felix quickly. "It's like I told you. You're seeing a magical illusion. Everything here is perfectly normal. For a place with an enchanted disease, that is."

A new voice echoes in from behind us. "Mack! So glad you're here."

Turning around, I see Roman march into the chamber, his gray hair in disarray.

I bow my head. "My Liege."

"Do you have any discoveries for me?" asks Roman.

Sure enough, Ace stalks in behind Roman. I wonder if the guy follows our Liege into the bathroom, too.

I gesture toward the cots. "When I walked in here, I saw what looked like red ghosts over the patients. What do you know about that?"

"Ghosts?" Roman's mouth falls open. "Are you all right? Why would there be red ghosts?"

Ace slips up behind Roman. "I told you. This mission is too much for Mack. You should let me go after the Essence."

"That won't be necessary," says Roman. "I'm sure

Mack is here with good news." Roman stares at me expectantly.

I narrow my eyes and think things through. There are two ways this could go. One, I push Roman on the red ghost situation. That won't go anywhere. If anything, Ace could use it as an excuse to try and elbow his way into my mission with the Halcyons. Two, I could give Roman a quick update and leave, fast.

Option two it is.

"I do have news for you," I state. "We should have the Essence for you in a few days."

"He's lying again," declares Ace. "If you're really going to the Halcyon den, then I should join you."

Kaps has been quiet this time, but just because she's silent, that doesn't mean she isn't thinking everything through.

The princess steps up to Ace. "Look, Buddy. Mack and I are getting the Essence. You are staying here."

Ace scowls. "Who is this? What's she got to do with anything?"

Pure rage heats my veins. I deal with Ace because I have to. But Kaps doesn't deserve any of his attitude.

Roman frowns. "I thought we talked about this, Mack. No emotions. No entanglements."

Kaps twiddles her fingers at Roman. "Beware, for I am tangly."

Okay, that was pretty good.

As I fight the urge to grin, my white-hot rage cools. The reason I came to the Fortress was to check on my fellow zoetic, not spend quality time with Roman and his human barnacle, Ace.

"We're leaving," I declare.

"What?" Roman gives me the sort of pleading face that would suit on an old hound dog. "You aren't off to your *refuge*, are you?"

Both Ace and Roman hate the fact that I have my own place nearby. Mostly because I've magically warded it so well, they've never been able to find it.

I look to Kaps. "Ready?"

"Ever so much."

And so we leave Ace and Roman behind.

43

KAPS

*M*ack and I stroll along the beach. Our destination? What Roman called Mack's *refuge*. I have dozens of questions about the situation and a nice setting to ask them, so I launch right into my mini-interrogation.

Learned a lot, actually.

Where did Mack get his refuge? From a senior citizen who got saved from vampire-related death.

How can the place be a walk away from the Fortress and yet no one knows where it is? Mack collects magical artifacts, same as I do. Turns out, he found a magical *warding stone of confusion* which protects his property. I want one.

I push for details on what his place looks like, but Mack is pretty cagey. All he'll say is that I'll *see for myself soon enough.*

Voices and music echo in from further on along the beach. Someone humans must be having a party. A familiar tune carries on the air.

> *Gray or green or brown or yellow*
> *Your look could change just like the rainbow*
> *I wouldn't care*
> *It's what we share*
> *You're mine*

It's a song written by Zin and Rhodes. I picture them swimming and chatting as they worked on their latest creation. As a matter of fact, it's not unlike how Mack and I were gabbing just now. But this isn't real life.

Mack isn't my rhana.

I picture the sick zoetic in their healing chamber. Mack could lose so many people. It's a weight that surrounds him, invisible and omnipresent.

And I lost someone, too. *Zin.* Even though my sister returned, the hurt still rattles around my soul somewhere. For her part, Zin seems totally happy and recovered. Not me. I'm still broken somehow. And hiding behind different masks.

Lone Vigilante.

Family Fuck Up.

Rock Chick.

That must be why I felt such a quick connection with Mack. Right away, we both recognized each other's pain. That could also be why I lost it when the SUV turned over. After all, I've saved plenty of humans before, but I've never spontaneously changed into a dragon along the way.

A memory appears: Great M's igni saying one thing, over and over.

She fights for Mack.

Maybe I do fight for him. Which is weird, considering how he's human while I'm a dragon shifter. There's no chance for us and romance.

A voice in the back of my head points out that I'm just making up excuses. After all, my buddy Rhodes' mother is human while his father is a dragon shifter. Stuff like that happens all the time.

Maybe I'm avoiding something. Or running. Or avoiding and running at the same time, which is very tricky to do, especially when you're swapping out characters along the way.

Argh. This is so confusing.

44

MACK

Kaps and I lounge on my L-shaped leather couch. Before us, a spread of Chinese food containers cover the low table.

It's a lot of dinnertime chewing and *not talking*.

Something is up.

Kaps shot off tons of questions on the beach. I figured she'd ask even more at the house. Especially since my place is a sprawling one-story ranch whose walls are decorated with bookshelves or drawers filled with relics, same as Kaps' lair.

But the princess has been silent. All of sudden, I know why.

"You've been quiet ever since that song," I offer.

Kaps pokes her chopsticks into a container with extra vengeance. "What song?"

"The one by Zin E. Ah. That's your sister, isn't it?"

"Sure." Kaps sets the container back on the table. "I'm not so hungry any more."

Getting the princess to talk is like trying to cradle a wildflower and a lightning bolt.

Hard to hold both.

Yet valuable when you do.

I focus on Kaps again. "After you saved me from the audax, things changed between us. We got connected somehow." Kaps stares at her hands. "I know you sense it, the same as I do. Talk to me. Please."

Long seconds tick by before the princess speaks. "When I was little, I liked going down to the royal treasury to look for relics. It was a game. Then Zin was taken. Kidnapped."

"That's terrible." *And I mean it.*

"Afterward, my parents wouldn't let me leave their side. Same with Huntress. But the last thing I wanted was to be protected. Nope, I ached for a fight. Then I found my first *El Dorado Adventures* comic in the treasury, and I was hooked. Audax... I could take them down in a way that I couldn't fight what had happened in my life."

Kaps turns to meet my gaze. "I asked my parents about the audax. They got so worried, they put guards outside my door. So I told my parents I wanted to play music like Zin. That went over well. Over time, I built up this rock chick persona and played music on Earth. Of course, the gigs were all located in places where I could find magical relics or kill audax."

I nod slowly, taking it all in. "That's why they want to believe you're not responsible."

"I call it being the Family Fuck Up, but *yes*, that's exactly it."

"As long as you're a troublemaker, then they think you're safe from worse threats."

"Right. At the same time, I also made up this other self, the Lone Vigilante. She fights audax and pads her pockets with new relics." Kaps' eyes glisten with sadness. "Now I have Rock Chick, Family Fuck Up and Lone Vigilante. There's no *me*."

"I disagree. There's so much more to you than that. And no matter how long it takes, I'll stay at your side until you realize how amazing you truly are."

The ghost of a smile rounds Kaps' mouth. "I could get a magical restraining order for that."

"What?" I wink. "I'll just follow you around, that's all. And watch over you while you sleep. Plus, maybe buy you extravagant gifts with hidden cameras inside."

Her smile widens. "This is all very specific stuff."

I bob my brows. "I watch the Hallmark channel in my spare time. Just to learn what *not* to do in real life."

"Thanks, Mack."

"Any time. I mean it. I owe you one."

"For saving you from audax? That's just what I do."

"No, for something bigger. Over the last year, I just got burned out inside. Nothing bothered me any more. It's like I could find a relic or step out into traffic, both were equally unappealing." I shift my body to face her. "I have you to thank for changing that."

"Me?"

"I'd been living in a black and white world for so long. Then I saw you dancing at the club, and you were everything alive and vibrant. I started to feel again. You changed me."

When Kaps next speaks, her voice is so low, I can barely hear her. "It's supposed to be like that with rhanas."

"Rhanas?"

"Life mates between dragons. Being around your rhana gives you strength."

"Humans have something like that, too. *Love at first sight.* And I do think some folks are just so similar, they understand the other person right away. Maybe more like *recognition at first sight.*"

Kaps blushes. "You saw me dancing; that's not exactly knowing me at my worst."

"True. Your worst took me a little while to discover."

Kaps looks at me, wide eyed. "What is it?"

"You don't believe in yourself, Kaps. You made a fake persona that your family believes. Now you accept it, too."

"Not everyone buys it. Great M is a holdout. She says I'm like her. But she's wrong. Great M's afraid of nothing. If something bad comes her way, she takes it down with a grin. That's not me."

"I can see the similarity. From what you say, neither of you stop. Maybe your Great M moves forward with a grin, and you do it while worrying, but you both fight."

Kaps starts to shift toward me, but stops herself. "Thanks, Mack."

"Like I said. Any time."

Kaps sits up straight, her legs bouncing with nervous energy. "And we still have the Halcyons tomorrow. I'll never fall sleep tonight."

"I have a secret system for chilling out before I go to sleep. Want to see it?"

"Sure."

Kaps scooches a little closer to me on the couch, and I take that as a very good sign indeed.

45

KAPS

*S*ecret system for getting a good night's sleep before a mission? Count me in.

Mack pulls a wireless keyboard from a side table. He types quickly across the keys. "Here you go."

The wide screen across from the couch shows different views of the Fortress.

"Ah, you tapped into the Fortress' security cameras."

"Bingo. Hours of fun." He clicks a few keys and brings up the healing chamber.

I point to the screen. "There's that Felix guy. What's he doing?"

"I can't really zoom in, but at this time of day, he'll be giving the patients their nutrition injection. It hydrates them, too."

A memory appears. "What were those red ghost things we saw in the healing chamber?"

"Good question." Mack clicks more keys. In the bottom-right hand corner, there's the time stamp for when we visited the healing chamber. 3:32 PM. The video shows Felix doing his rounds. And nothing else.

I frown. "Shouldn't that show us entering the chamber?"

"It should." Mack's hands fly across his keyboard once again. On screen, the video feed of the healing chamber goes super-fast. Within a minute, it's clear what's happening.

"The video is on a loop," I point out. "That's not a live feed. Did they do that everywhere in the Fortress?"

"One way to find out." Mack clicks more keys. A fresh image comes onto the screen: a mess hall. It's a large space made of gray stone. Long wooden tables line the floor. Mack goes through the same thing that happened with the healing chamber footage. Namely, he speeds up the video. This time, it's a very different situation.

"This isn't a loop," says Mack.

I scratch my cheek and consider things. "Felix whispered something about not upsetting Roman. Do you think that's what's going on?"

"Roman does have access to these same feeds, so

that's possible." Mack leans back and drums his hands on his kneecaps. "There's no time now to go back to the Fortress and check this out. I'll have to look into it tomorrow after we get the serum."

I move even closer to Mack, just because he's warm and this place is cold at night. And Mack's upper arm looks very cushy, so I lean against him for just a second.

"How about you show us something that's really boring?" I ask. "That might help us both get sleepy."

Mack shoots me another sly smile. This one makes my insides all squirmy. "You'll love the parking garage."

And you know what? It is rather soothing.

46

MACK

hile I flip through more video feeds, Kaps cuddles up beside me. Mission *Relax Kaps* is going well. I curl my arm up her back and run my fingers up her neck. Her hair is silken soft under my touch. I gently twist and unwind the strands between my fingers.

Kaps lets out a low *mmm* noise, so I assume my efforts are working well.

"That's nice," says Kaps. "What's it for?"

"Consider it a thank you for telling me so much about your sister and your personas. I know that isn't easy."

Kaps' mouth winds into a sleepy smile. "I was going to ask for popcorn, but now that you're playing with my hair so nicely, I don't seem to want any."

"Good."

Hours pass. Eventually, Kaps' breathing slows as she falls asleep beside me. Something deep within my soul is beyond pleased to have her at my side while she rests. A single thought echoes through my mind.

I'll protect you, my dragon.

KAPS

*a*t some point, I start to snooze on Mack's very cushy arm. Once I start to dream, I find myself standing in a landscape that's nothing but waist-high white clouds. A bright azure sky arches overhead.

Before me, a puff of cloud stretches into a familiar shape.

"Hey, Great M."

"Kaps." Great M's tail waves at me over her shoulder. "My igni tell me you've got a big day tomorrow. I came here with just one thing to say. Kick ass. I believe in you. Okay, that's two things. But you get the idea."

"I do. Thanks."

Great M winces. "Oh, I hear you." No question who *you* is in the scenario. *Igni.* "I already told her to kick ass."

"They're still freaking out, huh?"

"Right now, my head is a noisy place to be."

Frustration corkscrews up my back. *When it comes to these igni, enough is enough.* No one screams in my Great M's mind.

I cup my hand by my mouth. "Look, little lightning bolt guys. You need to stop chattering in my Great M's head and *do* something that actually helps me."

There, that told them.

Suddenly, the landscape fills with tiny lightning bolts. Igni whirl and dive in small clusters. It's like the air is filled with electronic schools of fish.

Whoa.

My eyes almost bug out of my head. I talked to the igni, but I didn't expect them to actually listen. Maybe the rules are different while you're in a dreamscape? Who knows.

A line of igni break free to swirl around my fingers. Lightning flashes around my arm. When the brightness vanishes, a ring of blue metal glimmers on my right hand.

Great M float-walks closer. "That's new."

I hold up my hand. "Your igni have never made a ring before?"

"Nope." Great M pops the 'p' on the word nope. That means she's absolutely serious.

"What do you think this ring does?"

"I'll check." Great M squeezes her eyes shut. "Little ones, can you give me the 411 on this ring?" She pops her eyes open. "Well, that was just a bunch of screech, screech, screechity screech. Total nonsense."

"I don't know how you manage all those noises in your brain."

"Very carefully." Great M raises her pointer finger. "Oh, wait. I'm getting actual words now." She exhales. "Okay, thanks for nothing."

"What did they say?"

"They say the magical ring is a for one-time use."

"Ah, that would be the *thanks for nothing* part of your conversation." *Most magical rings work that way.*

Great M slaps her hands against her ears. "Gah! They're at it again." She winces. "That's better, little ones. Thanks for real this time."

"What is it?"

"My igni say, *you'll know what to do with the ring when the moment is right.*"

"Not to be picky, but that's still not very specific."

"Once your grandfather got magically dragged off into oblivion and the only clue I got from my igni were the words *mirror man.*"

"So this is a lot of chatter for them."

"An incredible amount. But you're my mostly

favorite granddaughter, so let me try again." She closes her eyes again. "Little ones? Are you still there?" Great M scans the room. "I got nothing. Sorry."

"It's cool, thanks for trying." I give the ring a closer look. An image gleams out from the top of the band. "This is a sweet ring with a—" I purse my lips, looking for the right words "—a cute alien face on it."

"Oh, that's no alien. That's Iggy."

"Who?"

Great M opens and closes her mouth a few times. "Huh. I take it back. A cute alien is probably the best way to explain things."

The finger where I wear my new igni ring where I usually place my royal signet band. At that thought, a weight of guilt settles into my bones.

"How are Mum and Da?" I ask.

"Worried. Scheming. They've called in your Great Grandfather Xavier to do some research."

Grandpa Xav is an archangel who's been around since the dawn of time. "What's he doing?"

"Your Grandpa Xav has a lot of contacts,. Everyone owes him a favor. Let's just say I'm glad that whatever you're doing, it will happen tomorrow."

"Do I even want to know what they've planned?"

"Hey, I'd tell you if I had any ideas. I'm Great Scala Non Grata right now. The top of everyone's hate list."

I twist my hands together at my waist. *Grandpa Xav is in the mix?* This is seriously bad. Then I picture all those sick zoetic in the Fortress.

They need help. That's all that matters.

I straighten my spine. It doesn't matter who's after me. This is my life and my choice. I'm saving the zoetic. And Mack, too.

I round on Great M. "Tomorrow is a done deal. I've got this."

Great M punches the air with her fist. "That's my fave grand baby."

Suddenly the clouds grow so thick about me, I can't see my hand in front of my face. Next the white haze vanishes as my thoughts return to a far more regular type of dream. I'm now performing on stage in a green jumpsuit covered in porcupine quills. Overall, I look like a cactus.

I guess the dreamscape with Great M is over. A regular night vision has begun.

And in this new dream, the crowd goes wild.

MACK

*B*oth Kaps and I fall asleep. Yet some time during the night, we move around on my massive couch.

I know this because when I wake up, we're spooning. Kaps' head is cradled against my arm. She's thrown one leg over my hip. Every so often, she mumbles a little and smiles.

I lay silently, watching Kaps' eyes flutter under her lids.

Holding her close.

Keeping her safe.

What a perfect moment.

KAPS

I awaken in Mack's arms. It's a pretty nice situation. We're cuddled up face-to-face on his mega couch. Meanwhile, a very awake Mack diligently runs his fingertips along my cheek. I think he might be trying to brush hair away from my face, but I'm not sure.

I definitely don't care. The touching is nice.

Also, all the brushing of skin is accompanied by looks of quiet adoration. I wish we didn't have to go find a witches' coven, because I could do this all day.

Just as allies, mind you.

Hair maintenance is key part of any mission.

When Mack speaks, his voice is all low and growly. "What did you dream?"

"Why?" My stomach sinks. "Was I yelling in my sleep?"

According to Zin and Huntress, I do that sometimes.

"No, you were more twitchy and smiley."

"Oh, that." I exhale. "I saw Great M in something called a dreamscape. She wished us good luck."

Mack nods toward my hand. "Looks like it was more than a dream."

I hold up my hand and, sure enough, the ring from the igni is still there. "Yay! That was real." I flip my hand, Beyonce-style. "It's my *cute alien ring of randomness.*"

Mack leans in for a better look. "The image on the band is unusual. Does this alien have a name?"

"Iggy, I think."

"And what does this ring do?"

"I have no idea. All I got was, *when the time comes, I'd know how to use the ring.*"

"Sounds cryptic." He grins, and I realize I'm in deep trouble.

Because he's still doing that face-touching thing.

With those adoring blue eyes.

And last but not least, we keep spooning on this overly large piece of furniture. Who buys couches this big anyway? It's like the size of bed, really. That's unfair. It encourages premature snuggling with people that you've only just decided could join you on a very imper-sonal and totally professional mission of mercy.

Best to get some distance here.

I sit upright. Mack rolls onto his side and props his head on his hand. The movement highlights his upper arms, which are rather ripped.

Focus, Kaps.

"The dreamscape was nothing, " I begin. "Wait until you hear what happened after that. I dreamed that I was rocking out in this green costume with porcupine quills sticking out of it. Like I was cactus girl or something. The audience went nuts for it."

"That's not a surprise. It's a little bit of you in real life, isn't it?"

Screwing up my mouth to one side of my face, I think that through. Mack does have a point. I am a little bit of cactus girl. I strut around and sing for people who I never want to get very close.

"How did you figure that out?" I ask.

"I'm the same way, I guess." He grins again. The smile is so genuine and sweet, it takes my breath away. It also inspires a quick inventory of the situation.

I'm a dragon.

Mack is human.

I'm royal.

He's not.

I'm super committed to slaying audax and avoiding intimacy.

Mack is a very good kisser.

My logic is running sideways here. *Danger!* All in all, there's only one thing to do in a situation such as this one: Get the Hell off the couch and prepare for my mission.

So that's exactly what I do.

MACK

*K*aps zooms off the couch so quickly, you'd think she sprouted wings.

My girl dreams of being a cactus.

Yet she's all wildflowers and lightning bolts to me.

I adore her.

And I meant every word that I said last night. There are humans who don't believe in love at first sight, but I'm not one of them. After all, I run across magic very day. And meeting this amazing woman simply pulled me out of a void. I was lifted up just by knowing someone like her could exist in this world.

We can start off as two people who just happen to be on the same mission. Not a problem.

For Kaps, I'll be a patient man.

51

MACK

*N*ow that we're both awake, it doesn't take long for me and Kaps to get dressed. For today's mission, I wear black body armor. After all, who knows what will happen once I toss the ingot into the ocean? The Halcyons weren't exactly specific. For her part, Kaps wears her cargo pants and vest along with a hefty pair of boots. As a dragon shifter, her scales act as natural armor.

We're ready.

Kaps and I step away from my beach house and onto the golden sands. Waves gently roll onto the shore. A dark ocean stretches as far as the eye can see. The sky lightens.

Dawn is almost here.

Kaps and I stand ankle-deep in the surf. Water laps

around my boots. My gaze fixes on the horizon line. Electric excitement charges through my limbs.

I picture Ndidi and all the other zoetic. Their lives depend on this moment.

At last, the edge of the sun peeps over the horizon. I reach into my pocket and grasp the ingot.

Please, let this work. We must get to the Halcyons and find the serum.

Raising my arm, I toss the ingot into the waves.

Then we wait.

52

KAPS

*M*ack just tossed the magical ingot thingy into the water.

And nothing happens.

Minutes slowly tick by. And I do means slowly. Still, there's no sign of the Halcyon's den.

The sun rises half-way over the water. Mack and I exchange a worried glance.

What if that comic book wyvern was wrong? It's not like I have tons of experience with magical creatures made from paper.

The sun blares out from the sky, round and full. Dawn is over. My shoulders slump.

I turn to Mack. "I can always sneak us back into Furonium again. Maybe there's something we missed from the comic books."

Mack shakes his head. "There's no way I can ask you to return home so soon. You'll become a prisoner. I simply can't allow that."

"What about Gage?" I ask. "Maybe he has another artifact that can help."

A great roar of waves sounds, breaking up our chat. Turning, I see that the waters have risen to take the shape of a great wyvern. This time, the creature has a traditional dragon-style head. Its torso lifts from the ocean, with its massive wing-arms extended beneath it.

We step closer. Under the water-wyvern, a liquid tunnel opens into the ocean proper. It's a column of air within the churning dark waters of the Atlantic.

The water-wyvern swings its massive head in our direction. Dark eyes fix on Mack. No words are spoken, but it's clear what the thing wants.

Enter here.

"You still up for this?" asks Mack.

I shoots him a deadpan stare. "Are you kidding?"

Mack grins in reply. And so, side by side, we march into a supernatural tunnel that stretches under the waves.

53

MACK

Kaps and I march through the long tunnel. All around us, water swirls in a corkscrew motion. We step along until the passage opens up into a wide, oblong chamber made from shifting water. It strikes me that this must be what it's like to stand inside a soap bubble.

In the center of the space wait three figures. *The Halcyon witches.*

Two are human woman who are dressed in golden robes. Both have wyvern features. The first has a dragon's head. The second has wyvern arms, complete with side wings that connect to her torso.

The third Halcyon is massive, wyvern-sized creature with a supernatural body and a human woman's head. She's the one we met in Kaps' lair.

I bow my head slightly. "Hello, Ratna."

The massive wyvern tilts her head. "How do you know my name?"

"We saw you in Furonium," explains Kaps. "When we placed all the *El Dorado Adventures* comic books all together."

"Ah," says Ratna. "Some human artists must have siphoned off Halcyon magic. What you saw with the comic books was an echo of our power. Why are you here?"

"My people are sick," I explain. "They need the Essence."

The Halcyon witches exchange a series of looks. At last, Ratna speaks again. "We began life as human cartographers, the three of us. All the men were away for World War I, so we were sent to Florida to draw the coastline and found El Dorado instead. Our trio walked in as human and we left as the Halcyon coven. You can understand why we hide."

Kaps nods. "Some things even supernaturals don't understand."

"For years, we brewed potions to heal ourselves and return to our human form," continues Ratna. "It did not work. Over time, we learned that our changes brought along certain benefits. We three wield the power to create potions, see the future and inspire artists. Wonderful boons indeed. And so we are at peace."

Ratna looks between her fellow witches once more. Their eyes glow with golden light. "My fellow witches and I have just considered your request."

"And what do you say?" I ask.

"The zoetic are not ill. But we three agree. Giving you the Essence will heal them all."

I exhale. "Thank you. Where is the Essence?"

Ratna shifts her weight, making her front claws dig into the liquid floor. "The serum you seek lies at the other end of a question. Answer me truthfully, and the Essence is yours." Ratna's vertical pupils narrow as she glares in my direction. "Who are you?"

Easy enough.

"I'm Mack Valtas."

"No," says Ratna.

I rub my neck and consider things. When I was a baby, my human parents dropped me off at the Fortress. It's true that I don't know my real name. *What can I say that's true?*

"I repeat," says Ratna. "Who are you?"

"A human," I reply.

Ratna slams her front claw onto the floor, sending a spray of water into the air. "NO! I shall ask you one last time. WHO ARE YOU?"

Tension fills the air. *There's a trick here. There always is with witches.*

Kaps steps forward. "I can answer."

"Please do," says Ratna.

Pride and worry battle it out inside me. I'm beyond amazed that Kaps just volunteered here. But what if she answers wrong and there is a price to be paid?

I move to stand between Ratna and Kaps. The zoetic are my people. If there is punishment to be meted out, I'll take it upon myself.

KAPS

*O*kay, stepping forward wasn't my most thought-out plan. Still, I'm here and I'll work it.

I lift my chin. "He is my..." I swallow past the suddenly huge lump in my throat. "Partner. We go on, you know, adventures together."

My face blazes red. *Where did that some from? It's a very relationshippy statement.*

"Repeat that," says Ratna slowly.

I gesture toward Mack. "He's my adventure partner."

There, that sounded confident.

Radna's irises glow with golden light. It's a little unnerving, considering how she's just glaring and not saying anything.

At last, Ratna speaks again. "That answer, at least, is true."

Yellow light flares at Mack's chest. When the brightness fades, a vial of golden fluid hangs from a chain about his neck.

I wish I could be all *happy sunshine girl* here. But to be honest, I'm a little peeved. I get that Mack is zoetic. But there seems to be an ongoing theme of favoritism in the cool relic department. He got the ingot *and* the vial of Essence, which means one thing. The next goodie is mine.

"One drop is all anyone requires," says Ratna. "And now you may go."

And the water collapses all around us.

55

MACK

The oblong chamber begins to contract. I grab Kaps' wrist and run for it. Water closes in. Just as we reach the passageway's end, the tunnel collapses altogether.

Kaps and I rush off in the direction of the Fortress. As we jog along, I can't help but ask a question. "So, I'm your partner in adventure now, eh?"

A pretty blush crawls up Kaps' cheeks. "Yes."

"I'm new to this whole *adventure partner* dynamic. What's allowed?"

"Huh?"

"Do adventure partners hold hands?"

Her blush deepens. "Sometimes."

"Anything else?"

Kaps stares at my mouth and shivers. "Nothing I can think of."

"We'll work on that later."

And we will. But for now we'll get the Essence and save the zoetic.

56

KAPS

*M*inutes later, Mack and I rush up the front steps to the Fortress. We head straight the healing chamber. A red haze hangs in the air. The many sick figures on the cots writhe and moan.

My heart lurches in my chest. All the people in this room have dedicated their lives to saving humans. Now they lay in an enchanted sleep, moaning in pain.

Please, let this work.

Mack makes a beeline for his friend, Ndidi. As I speed past the cots, it's clear that the bloom has changed a lot since we last visited. Before, the red haze sat just over the patients' bodies. Now it's solidified into what looks a transparent shell that surrounds them from head to toe.

From the corner of my eye, I see those casings

change even further. For a moment, another face seems overlaid on the real human one. I shake my head and look again. The illusion of a red mask is gone.

A shiver runs up my spine. What's happening to these zoetic anyway? All the more reason to get them some healing serum and fast.

Mack kneels beside Ndidi's cot. The movement is so smooth, it's clear that this is something that Mack has done many times. My insides twist with grief. Ndidi is essentially the only family Mack has.

Gently raising his arm, Mack sets his palm on Ndidi's forehead. "You'll be fine, friend. I have a potion here to help you heal." Mack grips the vial and tries to pull the stopper out. His hand shakes so badly, it isn't easy.

I move in closer. "Let me."

Mack nods. I pull the stopper from the vial, revealing an eye-dropper device that's attached inside the lid.

Clever idea, Halcyons.

I lift the dropper just above Ndidi's mouth. A single golden bead falls onto his lips. Yellow light erupts from the spot. Clearly, the magic is working.

After resetting the lid onto the vial, I keel beside Mack. Nervous energy careens through my limbs. Ndidi lies before us, immobile.

Come on. Wake up.

Minutes pass. There's no change in Ndidi. Golden light shone; that means the magic got to work. But it doesn't seem to be healing Ndidi.

"Maybe it needs more time," I offer.

The muscles in Mack's neck tighten. "Roman showed me some tests he did with this serum. It wiped out any pathogen in seconds."

My mind races. There must be a step here that we skipped. After all, we talked to a comic book wyvern-human who led us to a bubble room under the ocean.

What did we miss?

Ace saunters back into the healing chamber, pausing beside Ndidi's cot. Mack's gaze stays locked on his best friend.

"Not working, is it?" asks Ace.

Little by little, Mack raises his gaze to focus on Ace. "What do you know about it?"

Ace rubs the gray stubble along his chin. "I should be the senior paladin here. Instead, I've got to follow around some nineteen-year-old kid."

Mack slowly rises to stand. "That's Roman's call."

"Roman made me take a magical vow not to hurt you, did you know that? Our Liege doesn't think you stand a chance against me, one to one." Ace's mouth twists with disgust as he scans the cots all around.

A realization appears. *This is no mysterious illness.*

The same thought must occur to Mack, because he now balls his hands into fists. "What did you do, Ace?"

"A lot," responds Ace. "Roman needed to see how important I was, so I put some runt zoetic to sleep."

I rise to stand beside Mack. "I saw red masks on these patients here. The new faces didn't look at all human. You did that, didn't you?"

Ace glares at me. "Mack got all the good missions. Roman sends me out to collect blood samples. That's drone work, dragon girl. So sure, I went on missions for blood samples, only I brought back demonic blood from my kills. A different one for each zoetic."

My eyes widen. Shock zings through my nervous system. "You can't go around pumping up humans with demon blood. That makes them open to…" I can't seem to for myself to say the word.

"Possession," finishes Ace.

A foul taste creeps up my throat. Every so often a human gets the not-so-bright idea to get possessed by a demon. It's a messy and painful process.

But here Ace forces possession on his fellow zoetic? What the ever loving Hell?

Mack rounds on Ace. "What is wrong with you?" Mack's voice strains with barely held-in rage. "Getting possessed is excruciating. Once the demon takes over, it always finds a way to shred the human's body. And you did this to thin out the ranks? Now you think Roman will pat you on the head and say you're his favorite?"

All the while, a figure rises behind Mack. It's Ndidi, or what's left of him. Mack's best friend shows a visage that's not entirely his own. A single eye glows red in his all-crimson face.

"Mack," I cry. "Watch out."

Mack pauses, sending the danger behind him. Little by little, he turns around.

"Whatever happens," says Mack in a low voice. "No one touches Ndidi."

Tilting back his head, Ndidi lets out an inhuman roar. Nearby, other patients writhe on their cots. The masks I saw before now solidify into new appearances.

The demons are taking over.

Demon-Ndidi leaps, swipes and punches. Mack dodges every attack. For his part, Ace stands by and simply watches, a gut-churning smile plastered on his face.

Focus, Kaps.

I force myself to think through options. Any second now, three-hundred or so demons will leap to life from their cots. Even in my dragon form, I can't take on that many. There's also no time to call in reinforcements. And leaving Mack alone to get killed is not happening.

A memory appears. I recall Ratna's words before she gave us the serum.

I wouldn't say the zoetic are ill. But we three agree. Getting the Essence will heal them all.

What if getting the Essence didn't heal the zoetic directly, but just revealed what was truly wrong with them?

I glance down at my hand. My new blue ring glimmers in the light. The igni always said I had to find the Halcyons. They never confirmed the serum would work, either.

But maybe this ring will do the trick.

After all, igni send souls to Heaven or Hell. I'm the granddaughter of the Great Scala. Somehow, I'm meant to be here. The igni said when the moment was right, everything would be clear.

And indeed, I know exactly what to do.

Suddenly, all the figures on the cots stand upright. Each zoetic now appears in shades of red as they take on the appearance of different demons. Some sport wings. Others have horns. Still more wield long talons. Adrenaline courses through me.

No time to lose.

Raising my arms, I speak to the igni in the way I've heard Great M do in the past.

"Come to me, my little ones!"

Thousands of small lightning bolts burst out from my ring. The many points of brightness zoom around the room. All the demons watch the shining movements, transfixed.

I issue a second command. "Open up Hell!"

Hundreds of igni speed toward the floor, where they spin about in a whirlpool shape. Soon that swirl lowers into the ground, reaching ever deeper.

All of a sudden, red light pours up through the new pit in the stone floor. Maybe it's just because I'm Great M's grandkid, but I know exactly what's happened.

The igni have reached Hell.

I call out my third command. "Surround the demons!"

These words send power zinging through my nervous system. Igni whirl about the room, surrounding each zoetic in a pillar of light.

These are soul columns, just like the one Great M used to send me to Earth. Only these demons aren't heading anywhere that pleasant.

The energy in my body turns so intense, it's as if my every cell were about to burst. I force out my final command.

"To Hell!"

The soul columns move, dragging out the red demon spirits from their human hosts. One by one, the columns spin down into the pit, delivering the demon ghosts back to Hell. Last to go is the demon that had possessed Ndidi. There's no missing that single eye.

A final blare of white light fills the chamber, followed by shadows and silence. The ring vanishes from my hand. All the zoetic collapse. They're alive, barely.

It is done.

Every inch of my body feels drained. It's all I can do to hunch over, brace my hands on my knees, and try to stay upright.

That's why I don't notice Ace running for me until it's way too late.

57

MACK

Seeing Kaps wield the power of the Great Scala took my breath away. But watching Ace leap for her?

My blood boils.

Lunging toward Ace, I rip the bastard away from Kaps. Raising my arm, I slam my fist right onto his jaw. That feels good.

Ace staggers back and whips out a weapon. *A Wurtzite dagger.*

This is the very weapon I was supposed to use to lure in Kaps. I swapped it out with a magical replica. Seems like Ace grabbed the real deal.

A Wurtzite dagger can cut through anything, including my body armor.

Not good.

Ace turns toward Kaps again.

Fresh waves of rage careen through me. A memory appears. The first time I kissed Kaps, connections formed deep within my soul. Now that sensation returns with a vengeance.

More energies align inside me. Greater cords of power whirl through my every muscle. All of a sudden, it's as if I can't contain the magic within. My body charges with an energy I don't know how to name. Even my skin tingles with power.

Rounding on Ace again, I pound into his kidneys with fresh fury. Ace staggers back before lunging forward again. He strikes his dagger straight into my tight arm.

I brace myself for the pain. That doesn't happen. My arm burns lightly, which means that wasn't a major strike. Or I'm too cranked up on adrenaline and it'll hit me later.

Still, the good news is that I'm not getting slowed down by the blow. I slam my shoulder into Ace's gut, and flip the guy over my back. Ace crashes onto the floor before jumping onto his feet. Once again, he brandishes the Wurtzite dagger.

This time, Ace stabs me right in the heart.

I gasp, waiting for the blade to cut right through my rib cage. It doesn't. There's some pain, sure. But the blade only digs about an inch into my skin. No further. It's almost as if my skin were covered in... I shake my head.

That can't be possible.

Ace pales. When it comes to the Wurtzite dagger, Ace seems just as shocked as I am. Seeing my opportunity, I twist the dagger out of Ace's hand. As the weapon tumbles away, I grab the blade in my own fist. Twisting Ace so his back is to my chest, I hold the Wurtzite blade against his throat.

"Move and you're dead," I declare.

My gaze immediately finds Kaps. She's still catching her breath after that amazing feat with igni. Yet she's safe.

Ace twitches under my grip. "You've ruined everything."

Roman marches into the healing chamber. He wears a white lab coat and a shocked look on his face. "What is this?" Roman pauses. "Step away from Ace."

Before, I felt power churning through me. Now that feeling returns. My thoughts move faster than ever before. Facts realign. Truths appears. And so I ask Roman the same question I got from the Halcyons.

"Who are you?"

58

KAPS

Who are you?

Mack's question reverberates through the chamber. Tension hangs thick in the air.

Roman smoothes back hair with his palms. With that simple motion, the man looks and acts like an entirely different person. Before, the guy always reminded me of a scatterbrained professor. Now he's more of an evil butler.

Roman scans the room. "Ace. Felix. I'm so disappointed in you both."

There's no missing how Mack still holds a dagger against Ace's throat. For the first time, I notice Felix cowering in a corner.

A sinking feeling settles into my bones. *What is Roman up to?*

For his part, Roman reaches under his white lab coat and pulls out a pair of small throwing daggers. With expert speed, he tosses the first weapon into Ace's chest. The second blade lands in Felix's stomach.

"Both of those blades are covered in poison," explains Roman smoothly. "You don't have long."

Ace and Felix wobble in place.

Then they both fall over, dead.

59

MACK

$\mathcal{D}$amn.

Ace and I weren't buddies, but the guy didn't deserve to die with a poisoned dagger in his chest. And what's the deal with Felix? The guy was a decent medic and now he's gone.

I round on Roman. "What is this?"

"You tell me," says Roman smoothly.

"You're not human," I declare.

"Closer." Roman keeps up his smug grin.

More bits of past realign. Roman studies blood obsessively, even though he never seems to discover anything useful. Perhaps that's because he's not researching to fight the audax. *He's working to help himself.*

"You're audax," I announce. "All that blood testing

was so you could perfect your glamour. That's why no one can see your true appearance."

Roman nods. "It took years to create blood additive that would fool even supernaturals into missing my true vampire nature. After that, I needed to become strong enough so I wouldn't require a full feeding every day. That meant drinking from thousands of humans. Yet I did. Next I had to drain enough blood from a single human donor. Then things became easy. Now I sip a bit each day from my stores to keep this form."

"That's why the blood storage is almost empty," I state. "It's not because there are no zoetic to bring in new samples. You're depleting your own stock of *whoever's face your wearing.* You've looked like this since World War II."

"Correct," says Roman, his fangs glistening.

"Why would you poison Ace and Felix?" asks Kaps. "Audax only kill for a meal."

"I am not *most* audax," says Roman. "Ace deserved to die. He was so jealous of Mack, the fool didn't see how he was doing my bidding."

This is a stunner. I always thought Roman and Ace were friends. Now I see that mu so-called liege actually hated the paladin.

Roman gestures across the healing chamber. "These are all runt zoetic that I wanted to destroy. Ace wanted to kill them as well, but for another reason: to gain my attention. What a fool. I allowed Ace to end them since it suited my purposes. But now that the runts are almost dead, it was time for Ace to die."

"And Felix?" I ask.

"The medic did what Ace asked," explains Roman. "Felix injected blood from different demons into each zoetic."

Kaps frowns. "So you wanted Ace to kill these zoetic because they're runts? What's that about?"

Roman shrugs. "There's a bigger plan at work here. Of course, neither of you see it."

A chill crawls up my neck as the truth appears. "You're the Elector."

Roman grins. "I was hoping you'd know the truth before the end. All I've ever wanted is to return to El Dorado. The city vanishes and appears at regular intervals. After World War II, I had to wait decades for the city to reappear. And every year, more amateur vampire hunters were cropping up."

Kaps nods. She knows all about vigilante vampire hunters.

"Audax numbers were dwindling," continues Roman. "So I came up with a plan. The best way to protect myself was to form my own opposition. I created the largest and most powerful anti-vampire army in the world. Now, the gates to El Dorado will soon reappear. And I am ready."

I force myself to process this truth. My Liege is the Elector. Once he gets into El Dorado, Roman will undoubtedly build up his army of audax once more. That means all of humanity is at risk.

"The other zoetic didn't run off, did they?" I ask.

"No, they're waiting to be transformed into my new army." Roman gestures across the healing chamber. "And these runts refused the chance to become immortal. That's why they all had to die."

All this while, my crew has been slipping closer to the chamber doors. I'm sure they mean to help, but none of them are wearing body armor or weapons. I glare at Jenna and shake my head slightly. She gets the message and convinces Dani and Zero to hold back.

"So the missing zoetic accepted your invitation to become vampires." I tilt my head. "Why not ask me?"

Roman chuckles. "After all these years, you still have no idea who you are and what you're capable of." Roman raises his fist. "It took months to get these runt zoetic ill with the so-called bloom. Ndidi was the hardest to make fall. But at last, I had you just where I wanted you, Mack. Alone and undefended."

Kaps steps forward. "Wrong."

"Precisely," says Roman. "You came in and blocked all my plans."

More pieces of the past realign. "That's why you warned me about attachments."

"Quite," says Roman. "I had to get rid of her. But how to stop a powerful dragon shifter? It took some doing, but I figured out a counter-attack. It meant that I would have to expose my true nature to you earlier than I wanted. Yet the most important thing is done. Your little dragon girl won't be a problem any more."

My skin crawls with unease. Suddenly, the skies darken, ending the beams of light that cascade through the square windows. A familiar sound follows.

The flapping of wings.

Oh, no. Dragons.

KAPS

Can that be?

Every cell in my body seems to freeze. The sound repeats, setting my nerves on edge. That's the beating of wings, all right.

Dragons are definitely on their way.

And by the intensity of noise, there are a lot of them, too.

An electric tension crackles through the air. I've felt this before, back when Mum cast the aegis web. No question in my mind. A spell is being cast.

Snap!

Above me, long fissures appear in the ceiling. Bits of stone and plaster tumble to the floor.

Crunch!

One end of the ceiling rips free from the walls. The

sense of magic grows even thicker. A cacophony of small explosions sound as the roof gets ripped off, the emotion reminding me of some giant rolling up a whacked-out carpet over our heads. More chunks of stone tumble to the floor. Dust fills the air.

When everything clears, the first thing I notice is Mum in her human form. She wears her red robes and a stern look on her face. And behind Mum, the skies are dark with a mixture of dragons and archangels in silver armor. Mum sits astride the largest dragon of them all: a great black beast.

That would be Da.

Mum focuses on me. "I see we arrived in time." She then points to Mack. "My magic leaves no questions. You tried to kidnap my daughter."

Oh, no.

Dragon-Da swings his head toward Roman. "Thank you for warning us, oh Zoetic Liege."

Roman bows his head. "Anything I can do to help."

Panic streams through my nervous system. Roman set this up. Somehow, the Zoetic Liege knew that Mack and I would connect. This has all been part of an elaborate scheme. Roman manipulated things so Mack ended up delivering me to Gage. I was supposed to stay in Furonium, but then I escaped. Next Roman cranked up my parents on this kidnapping thing.

I focus on Mum. "You've got it all wrong."

"He's not your kidnapper?" asks Mum.

I'd lie, but that would be pointless. "You don't understand. It's not like that anymore."

"But it was?" asks Da. "No one hurts my daughter."

Mack crumples over. Racing across the chamber, I kneel at his side. Every muscle in his body seems to strain as Mack grits his teeth in pain.

It's an immobilization spell. I've seen these before. The pain is so intense, it feels as if you're being turned inside out. I pat down my pockets. I must have some kind of relic to help Mack here.

Meanwhile, Roman calls toward my parents. "Our agreement remains, does it not?"

I pull out a *coin of healing* and set it onto Mack's hand. If it alleviates his pain, Mack doesn't show it. *Hells.* Mum is strong magic user. Undoing this spell won't be easy. Still, there are more things to worry about here than just Mum's magic.

"Agreement?" I call. "What's the price?"

It's Da who answers. "After we execute this evil human, Ace wants the body."

"No," I whisper.

The world seems to spin around me. Mack is in pain. He'll soon be dead. Something in my soul snaps. A realization slams into me.

All my life, I thought I chased audax. In truth, I've only been running away from my own life. In the same way, I thought I wore masks. Yet they only served to hide me from myself.

All that must end, now.

I'm done allowing my past fears keep me from the present reality. And a big truth confronts me right now. Still holding Mack's hand, I focus on my parents.

"Mum. Da. You can't do this. Mack is my rhana."

61

MACK

Pain sears through every nerve ending in my body. It's as if I'm being stabbed in a thousand places all at once. Yet Kaps' words still echo through my soul.

Mack is my rhana.

I'm human. Kaps is a dragon shifter. It's not possible that we're magically bound in this way. And yet, as soon as Kaps says the words, they feel true in my heart.

She's my rhana, too.

The woman in red robes—Kaps' mother—does not

seem impressed. "This human tried to kidnap you. Do not lie to us."

As if to accent this point, a fresh wave of agony moves through my body. I fight the urge to groan. Kaps is worried enough as it is. No need for her to know the levels of hurt I endure.

"That's only part of the story," Kaps focuses on the massive black dragon that her mother sits astride. "Please, Da. You knew Mum was your rhana the moment you saw her, didn't you?"

The emperor dragon keeps flapping his wings in a steady rhythm. Behind him, thousands of dragons and angels do the same. Some might think so many warriors is overkill, but if anyone were threatening Kaps and I had access to a legion of dragons and battle angels? I'd do the same thing.

The emperor swings his great dragon's head around, pausing when his gaze meets that of the empress. The pair share a long look. There's nothing said out loud, but I've no doubt that a great discussion is going on.

"He may live," declares the emperor at last.

Instantly, the pain drains from my body. I take in some deep breaths and regroup. This news is certainly good for me, but Roman won't be pleased. He's been working on this scheme for a while. Who knows how long my so-called Liege has been feeding the emperor and empress lies?

I scan the healing chamber. Roman isn't anywhere in my line of vision, but that doesn't mean he isn't lurking somewhere nearby. After today, I wouldn't put anything past him.

Beside me, Kaps runs her fingers through my hair.

"Are you all right?" she asks gently.

"Perfect."

Joy sparks in my chest. I meet her gaze and smile. In this moment, there are only two words to say.

"My rhana."

62

KAPS

*M*ack thinks I'm his rhana, too.

My heart soars. I press my lips to his. It's a spicy kiss, considering how my parents and half the after-realms are looking on. Yet I don't care.

"I love you," I whisper. "Find me again, bounty hunter."

Tendrils of magic wrap around me. Since it's Mum's power, it looks like red sparkly stuff. Normally, I'd think this power is pretty. Right now? Not so much. The supernatural cords pull me away from Mack. Every inch we move further apart feels like part of my soul is being torn away.

The magic places me onto Da's back, right behind Mum. From up here, it's quite a view. The roofless Fortress... the zoetic lying in haphazard ways across their white cots... and Mack lifting his gaze to meet mine. His voice carries on the wind.

"I will see you again, my rhana."

Da flaps his wings and takes back off toward a portal cloud. The warrior angels wing back toward Heaven.

And I return to my tower.

63

MACK

The great black dragon becomes smaller in the sky. Soon, Kaps is so far away, there's nothing but a small point of darkness to signify the entire dragon horde.

And then, nothing.

Emptiness fills my soul, yet I press the pain aside. I will find Kaps again. Turning about, I scan the healing chamber for Roman once more.

Jenna steps up. Dani and Zero follow closely behind her.

"Roman ran off," announces Jenna. "We tried to catch him, but he was too fast. We lost him, Liege."

There's a lot to process in those short statements. First of all, I'm happy my crew wasn't able to keep up with Roman. He's far too advanced for these three.

Second, there's the fact that Roman well and truly escaped, which means we'll have to hunt him down later. And third, there's how that Jenna called me her Liege. It's true I'm the ranking zoetic now, but it still feels strange to have the title.

"We heard everything that Roman said," adds Dani.

Zero sighs. "I can't believe Roman was a traitor all this time."

"Keep that secret for now," I state. "The other zoetic need to heal, not worry about Roman. Come along."

Grabbing the vial from around my neck, I head for Ndidi. He's sprawled on the ground, in the same position where he fell after Kaps released her igni.

"Zero, Dani," I command. "Get Ndidi in place." The pair quickly move to set Ndidi's body onto his cot.

My friend never looked so ill, even when he was stricken with the bloom. Or rather, the forced possession that Roman purposely misdiagnosed. Ndidi's skin now has a pale and crusty appearance. His once-bright eyes seem sunken into his skull, while his strong bone structure suddenly appears downright skeletal.

I open the glass vial and pull out the dropper.

Come on, Halcyons.

Once again, I give a single drop of serum to Ndidi. The golden liquid flares with magical light once it hits his lips. Instantly, the brightness spreads across his head and torso, then down his legs. Color returns to Ndidi's skin. His face takes on a less deathly look.

My friend opens his eyes a crack. "What happened to you?" he asks. "You look like Hell."

I can't help but smile. "Not much. How are you feeling?"

"Like an elephant has been tap dancing on my internal organs, but other than that, fine."

I pat his shoulder. "Good. Rest for now, my friend. I'll return once I've seen to the other zoetic."

"I want the full... once you..." Ndidi closes his eyes and falls back to sleep.

Turning, I face the now roof-free room with its three-hundred-plus sick zoetic.

It looks like the Essence will heal them, after all.

64

KAPS

THREE WEEKS LATER

Once again, I stand in a landscape of waist-high clouds. And Great M is here to chat.

"Is this working?" asks Great M.

"You got through," I reply.

"Oh, yay. Your Mum put some heavy duty spells on your tower. It's taken me a while to break in."

"She wants me to rest and recover from my traumatic experience."

"I heard." Great M purses her lips. "You don't look upset, though."

"I did what you said. Met the witches. Got the serum. Found my rhana. Maybe he's human, but it doesn't matter. He's mine."

"Good job, baby girl." Great M grins. "Tell me, how are things in the tower?"

"Nice enough. You know the place is more of a spa than anything else. I'm here with Huntress."

"Oh, how was her retreat?"

I shrug. "Complicated."

Great M frowns. "What happened to my favorite granddaughter? Who do I have to kill?"

"Huntress is fine, Great M. You don't need to kill anyone. I think my sister's adjusting to being my warden."

Which is true. Partly.

"Besides," I continue. "I thought I was your favorite granddaughter."

"You are." She tilts her head. "What? Sure. Got it. I'll tell her."

"Are your igni chattering away again?"

"Oh, yeah. My igni want you to know that they appreciate what you did. To them, this is the worst crisis they've ever faced. And that's saying something."

"Hey, we helped each other."

Great M stares at me for a long moment. "You've changed."

"Really?" I ask. "How so?"

"Sometimes, you would act a little—" she taps her chin "—what's the word?"

Huh. Maybe Great M noticed my Family Fuck Up persona. "Flighty?"

"That's it."

Oh, she noticed, all right.

"Other times you'd seem so incredibly serious," continues Great M. "Like a villain from a human James Bond movie."

"You're not wrong." I can't help but laugh. *That would be my Lone Vigilante self.*

"And in other instances, you were all about your music tours."

That would be Rock Chick girl. Great M calls it again.

"But now, you're different," says Great M. "I like it."

"I didn't know who I was before. But when I faced the idea of losing Mack? It pushed me to the limit. And I had boundaries that I didn't know were there to begin with. Does that make sense?"

"It does, Kaps. I'm so proud of you. What's next?"

"Mack and I will reunite, break into a magical city and kill us some vampires."

Great M pats under her eyes. "Oh, that's so romantic."

I laugh again. "Only you would say that."

"Oh, gotta go. Bye, Baby!"

With that, Great M's body turns back into clouds once more.

65

MACK

*a*nother day at the healing chamber. The hours are long, but I don't mind. It's important for folks to see their new Liege active and helping.

Was it only three weeks ago that I gave drops of Essence to every zoetic? Seems like another lifetime.

The zoetic are now healing. We even have a few folks who may be ready for active duty again soon. Which is good considering how the audax are definitely having a feeding frenzy these days. Roman's still out there, and clearly he's organizing more raids on humans.

The sooner we can start regular missions again, the better.

I sit by Ndidi's bedside and play at *war*.

The card game, that is.

Ndidi lays down his card. "You love this dragon girl?"

"I do." I set down my own card.

"So, when do you plan to tell me the truth?"

I chuckle. "There are multiple truths out there, Ndidi."

"I'm thinking about the one concerning your arm and chest?"

I set my cards aside. "When did you figure that out?"

"Oh, a little Jenna bird told me that she saw Ace stab you with a Wurtzite dagger. You're not dead. And these days, you always wear long sleeve shirts, no matter the weather."

"You're the best spy we have."

Ndidi scans from left to right. "No one's looking. Show me."

I don't need to tell Ndidi to keep this a secret. He really is the best spy in the zoetic. "All right." I roll up my sleeve. Just below my elbow begins a line of tough golden skin.

Dragon scales.

Ndidi purses his lips in a silent whistle. "Now how did you get those?"

"It's as Jenna told you. Ace tried to stab Kaps. I stepped in on took the blow instead. My body reacted." I roll my sleeve down again.

"And why would your body do that?"

"One reason only," I state. "To protect my rhana."

Ndidi sets his cards onto the side table. "You're giving me a headache with this mystery talk. I must rest now."

"Sure thing, Ndidi." I set my cards on to the table beside his. "We'll pick up the game later."

And one day, perhaps Kaps can play as well. After all, I have a rock-solid plan for breaking her out of that dragon shifter jail.

It's all a matter of time.

66

KAPS

*A*fter my dreamscape with Great M, I awaken in my tower bedroom. It's just past dawn and, per usual, Huntress is up already. She stands in the doorway.

"Good morning, Kaps," she says, unsmiling.

I toss a pillow at her head. She dodges it with ease. "You know, standing around and watching me sleep counts as stalker behavior."

"I'm your warden. It's my job to watch you."

"Only because you're the only person who can keep me locked up."

"True." Huntress shifts her weight from foot to foot. She never used to be the fidgety type. But that was before Gage Beaumont. "What do you want to do today?"

"We could garden again," I offer.

"You hate that."

"Yeah, but you look miserable, so I'm taking pity on you."

Huntress sighs. She's really got it bad. That makes me feel guilty for saying the *miserable* thing.

"I take it back," I say quickly. "You seem awesome."

Huntress crosses the room to sit at the end of my mattress. "I must see him again," she says solemnly. "Gage Beaumont, that is."

"Yeah, I kinda figured out that part." I sit up and wrap my arm around her shoulders. "Guess what? I must see Mack, too." I give her a gentle squeeze. "Let's escape, sister."

Huntress fixes me with a shocked stare. "I do not break the rules."

"Rules, shmules. Do you think you'll ever see Gage again if you do what everyone tells you to all the time?"

Huntress hugs her elbows. "No, I will not."

"Then let's scheme to get ourselves out of here."

A long pause follows before Huntress speaks again. "Yes, we will go."

I grin my face off. "That's the spirit." And in my heart, I add a silent vow.

Soon, my rhana.

-The End-

*Don't miss the epic conclusion to the story of Kaps and Mack.
Order MACK, Angelbound Offspring #6!*

ALSO BY CHRISTINA BAUER

MACK

Don't miss the epic conclusion to the story of Kaps and Mack. Order MACK, Angelbound Offspring #6!

HUNTRESS

The adventure continues with HUNTRESS, Angel-bound Offspring #7!

ANGELBOUND

Try ANGELBOUND, the kick-ass paranormal romance
with more than 1 million copies sold!

FAIRY TALES OF THE MAGICORUM

A modern fairy tale that *USA Today* calls a 'must-read!'
Check out WOLVES AND ROSES!

PIXIELAND DIARIES

PIXIELAND DIARIES tells the story of sassy pixie Calla and 'her' elf prince, Dare.

BEHOLDER

Medieval mages ... Slow-burn love ... And heart-pounding action! Check out the BEHOLDER series!

IF YOU ENJOYED THIS BOOK…

…Please consider leaving a review, even if it's just a line or two. Every bit truly helps, especially for those of us who don't *write by the numbers,* if you know what I mean. Plus I have it on good authority that every time you review an indie author, somewhere an angel gets a mocha latte. For reals.

And angels need their caffeine, too.

ACKNOWLEDGMENTS

If you're reading my freaking acknowledgements, chances are, I should thank you for something. So, for the record: you are awesome, dear reader.

That said, huge and heartfelt thanks must go out to my husband and son for their rock-solid support. Writing books means a lot of early mornings, late nights, long weekends, and never-ending patience. You two are the best guys in the universe, period.

After that, I must thank the extensive network of reviewers, friends and colleagues who helped me build my writing chops in general. Gracias.

Finally, deep affection goes out to my late, much loved, and dearly missed Aunt Sandy and Uncle Henry. You saw the writer in me, always. Thank you, first and last.

COLLECTED WORKS

Angelbound Offspring

The next generation takes on Heaven, Hell, and everything in between

Angelbound Origins

About a quasi (part demon and part human) girl who loves kicking butt in Purgatory's Arena

2. Scala

3. Acca

4. Thrax

5. The Dark Lands

6. The Brutal Time

7. Armageddon

8. Quasi Redux

9. Aquila

Angelbound Lincoln

The Angelbound experience as told by Prince Lincoln

1. Duty Bound

2. Lincoln

3. Trickster

4. Baculum

5. Angelfire

Fairy Tales of the Magicorum

Modern fairy tales with sass, action, and romance

1. Wolves and Roses

2. Moonlight and Midtown

3. Shifters and Glyphs

4. Slippers and Thieves

5. Bandits and Ball Gowns

6. Evil Queens and Goblin Kings

Pixieland Diaries

Sassy pixie Calla loves elf prince Dare. Too bad he hasn't noticed her. Yet.

1. Pixieland Diaries
2. Calla
3. Dare
4. Ley Queen

Dimension Drift

Dystopian adventures with science, snark, and hot aliens

1. Scythe
2. Umbra
3. Alien Minds
4. ECHO Academy

This is a completed series.

Beholder

Where a medieval farm girl discovers necromancy and true love

1. Cursed
2. Concealed
3. Cherished
4. Crowned
5. Cradled

This is a completed series.

ABOUT CHRISTINA BAUER

Christina Bauer thinks that fantasy books are like bacon: they just make life better. All of which is why she writes romance novels that feature demons, dragons, wizards, witches, elves, elementals, and a bunch of random stuff that she brainstorms while riding the Boston T. Oh, and she includes lots of humor and kick-ass chicks, too. Christina lives in Newton, MA with her husband, son, and semi-insane golden retriever, Ruby.

Stalk Christina on Social Media

Blog:
http://monsterhousebooks.com/blog/category/christin
a

Facebook:
https://www.facebook.com/authorBauer/

Instagram:
https://www.instagram.com/christina_cb_bauer/

Twitter:
@CB_Bauer

VLOG:
https://tinyurl.com/Vlogbauer

Web site:
www.bauersbooks.com

SUBSCRIBE

Get a FREE copy of Christina Bauer's novella, BEVERLY HILLS VAMPIRE, when you sign up for her personal newsletter:

https://tinyurl.com/bauersbooks

Not available in stores

BEVERLY HILLS VAMPIRE

A NOVELLA BY
CHRISTINA BAUER

AFTERWORD

Here are some behind-the-scenes facts about Kaps! In no particular order, they concern:

Wildlife

A tortoise does live in Central Park. His name is Henry. There is also a turtle pond in the park, but those creatures aren't really large enough to truly get a grip on a vampire's nut sack.

Nazis

During WWII, nazis actually landed in Florida. By some accounts, they did so more than once. I am also obsessed with WWII. I mapped out how the various nazi military arms would extend to the audax. All that ended up with one mention of how Carnage was a shock trooper.

Florida

I couldn't find any text that showed sightings of El Dorado in Florida, but a Spanish explorer named Ponce de Leon sought the Fountain of Youth in Florida, so I figured that it would work. Also, if any place contains a magical city that creates vampires, it's Florida. The state is a notorious vortex of the strange, and I mean that as a complement of the highest order.

El Dorado

From my reading, El Dorado is not a myth created by first peoples of South America. It's more of a tall tale spun by outsiders that basically says, *go to South America! The folks there have gold and you can steal it!*

This is very different from something like the Incan tale of the Ayar brothers. That one has cool stuff in it like a golden staff and one brother ascending to the throne. I've had it on my list to develop into a story for ages.

But back to El Dorado.

When adapting fairy tales, I try to keep to the essence of the story. With El Dorado, it's about looking at something new and—instead of respecting its beauty—seeing what can be taken for personal gain.

In writing Kaps, I began with this take on the myth of El Dorado, combined it with Florida and some Nazis and—*voila*—that's the back story for Kaps!

Why This Is Important (to me, anyway!)

For each book, I base the tale on a myth that relates to the main character's inner journey. Kaps is passionate about saving humans from audax. However, she doesn't really know what she's after. There's the golden city... and then there's what's really valuable. Kaps needs to figure her shit out. So does Mack for that matter but I can't say anything omre because of SPOILERS!

The whole El Dorado angle comes into a lot more focus in the next installment of this series, I can tell you that. In all honestly, I tried to jam everything into one book, but it simply didn't work. This story is really about the Halcyon coven and the zoetic. But the next book is all El Dorado, all the time!!!

There's so much more for us to discover and share

about Mack and Kaps. I can't wait to share it all
with you.

CB